A JEALOUS HEART

Faye has come to work at Monkshill, seeking peace after the trauma in her life, but she is unaware of the murderous events that have happened there. There is jealous rivalry between the two Montfort brothers who own Monkshill, and someone resents Faye being there and ruthlessly tries to drive her away with a series of upsetting events. Then she finds herself falling in love with her boss, Luke, who apparently views her only as his employee. It is not until tragedy strikes that Faye finds true happiness.

Books by Linda James
in the Linford Romance Library:

YIELD TO A TRAITOR

LINDA JAMES

A JEALOUS HEART

Complete and Unabridged

LINFORD
Leicester

First published in Great Britain in 2004

First Linford Edition
published 2005

British Library CIP Data

James, Linda
  A jealous heart.—Large print ed.—
  Linford romance library
  1. Love stories
  2. Large type books
  I. Title
  823.9′2 [F]

  ISBN 1–84395–793–0

Published by
F. A. Thorpe (Publishing)
Anstey, Leicestershire

Set by Words & Graphics Ltd.
Anstey, Leicestershire
Printed and bound in Great Britain by
T. J. International Ltd., Padstow, Cornwall

This book is printed on acid-free paper

1

Faye swept her shoulder-length hair from her face as she studied the map spread out on the dashboard. According to Mr Danby, who had interviewed her, when she reached the crossroads at Applewyke, she should take the road to the right, which led through Fossdale Moor. Monkshill was less than a mile from there. The entrance gates were apparently set back from the road, but could be seen quite clearly.

She hadn't seen any sign of habitation, nothing but lush green pastures with slopes gently rising in a pattern of dry-stone walls, interspersed with rocks of white limestone, thousands of years old. This was an ancient landscape, lost in the mists of time and one which Faye was eager to explore when time permitted. There was no time to admire the scene now. She was lost and realised she would have to go back to the crossroads and try a different direction.

She opened the car window, allowing a blast of cold air to rush in. It was March, but felt more like January in the strong biting wind. In the distance was a long line of dark hills, still topped with traces of the heavy snowfall which she'd heard had covered most of this part of Yorkshire in recent weeks.

Although Yorkshire born she had only briefly visited the North York moors in the past. She knew how beautiful it was and had jumped at the chance to work in the heart of the moors. It would she hoped begin a new chapter in her life, after having to put her life on hold while she looked after her terminally-ill mother.

Sadly her mother passed on after much suffering, and Faye realised she had to do what her mother wished and get on with her life. Flicking through a magazine one day, which held advertisements for nannies and housekeepers, catering etc., she saw the vacancy for a manager to run the Old Friary Tea Room within the grounds of Monkshill, a fourteenth-century house, built near to the ruins of a Benedictine Abbey.

Faye had previously owned a café, but as she had been out of the job market for several years she did not believe her application would be successful. When Mr Danby rang her the following day after her interview in Leeds and offered her the job, she could hardly believe it.

Faye took out the covering letter Mr Danby had sent her. Yes, she had followed his directions to the letter, but she had only succeeded in getting lost.

'We'll have to go back to the crossroads, Lucy.' The answering loud meow came from the basket on the back seat. Faye's cat was moving restlessly in her cage. It was a rather tedious journey from Hull for an animal to be cooped up in a confined area.

'I think we'd better stretch our legs first, my pet? Don't worry, we'll soon be in our new home.'

Lucy purred her thanks as her mistress fitted the harness and lead. They got out of the car and the little cat was happy to pad among the brown prickly bracken for a few minutes, sniffing daintily at various spots along the way.

After several minutes, Faye turned back towards the car. She huddled into her thick fleece jacket, steeling herself against the arctic wind which seemed to penetrate to her bones. She led Lucy towards the road, then in the distance she saw a vehicle was travelling at great speed in her direction. Perhaps they knew where Monkshill was?

She swept Lucy into her arms and ran, waving furiously as she did so. The driver of the car slowed down and pulled in behind her own car with a screech of brakes.

'Thank you for stopping,' she said, as the driver's window lowered. 'I hope you don't mind, but I've lost my way. Perhaps you may be able to direct me?'

A man, whom she judged to be in his late thirties, smiled up at her and Faye was immediately aware of the twinkling humour in his dark grey eyes. He glanced at Lucy, clinging to her shoulder.

'I'll try and help if I can. That's a funny looking dog you have there.' He gave a loud infectious laugh and Faye found herself laughing with him.

'I've travelled up from Hull today and she's rather fed up of being in her basket. I'm looking for a place called Monkshill. Do you know of it?'

The man's smile faded. 'Monkshill! Why do you want to go there?'

Faye was taken aback by his question. 'Is there any reason why I shouldn't?'

He stared at her for a long moment. 'I can think of several, which I won't go into. I'm sorry, it was very ill mannered of me to ask you your personal business. Are you going to work at Monkshill?'

'Yes, Mr Luke Montfort is employing

me to manage the Old Friary Tea-Room when it opens in April. Do you know the family?' she asked.

'You could say that,' he said with a wry twist to his lips. 'I'd better introduce myself. I'm Adam Montfort, Luke's elder brother. I no longer live at Monkshill, but I'm sure you'll hear the reason why eventually.'

'I'm pleased to meet you, Mr Montfort. I'm Faye Weston.'

'First names, please. We're not formal at Monkshill, that went out years ago, after Grandfather died.'

Faye placed her hand in Adam's outstretched one. 'Mr Danby mentioned at my interview that your brother suffers with rheumatoid arthritis. Does that hamper his ability to work?'

'Not so you'd notice,' he remarked in a dry tone. 'It only affects his hands at the moment but he won't give in and admit he has a problem. He can be a bad-tempered cuss, so be warned. He won't suffer fools gladly.'

'Well, I'll try not to be a fool,' she answered in a caustic tone. She wasn't sure she liked the image of Luke Montfort that his brother had conjured up.

Adam suddenly smiled, which made him look very attractive. Faye felt her heart lurch. Steady on, she thought. Haven't the lessons of the past taught you anything? You've just recovered from being badly let down by a man. Don't allow one smile to let you forget.

'I hope you like Monkshill, despite it being a creepy old place. The house and the ruins of the old abbey are reputedly haunted. Does that put you off?'

'I fear the living more than the dead,' she replied matter-of-factly.

'I'm glad you're not easily scared.' There was that devastating smile again. 'But I'd better warn you he won't like that!' He pointed to Lucy, who was observing him through half-closed eyes. 'I'm surprised he agreed to let you bring it!'

7

Faye's heart sank. She hadn't envisaged there would be a problem bringing her cat with her.

'I didn't mention I had a cat. I wouldn't have applied for the job if I'd known he had a disliking for them.'

'He hates them, but he'll probably give you a chance and if you prove good at your job, he may overlook it.'

Adam sounded grim, which made Faye begin to have further doubts about working at Monkshill. If he insisted Lucy couldn't stay, then neither would she. Surely the most important thing was being able to do her job well?

'I'm in rather a hurry. If you would like to get in your car, Faye, I'll lead the way to Monkshill.'

She did as Adam asked and soon found he drove much faster than she did. Lucy mewed in protest as Faye had to increase her speed considerably to keep up with him, and the car rode the hills like a fairground roller-coaster. She swore at the stupidity of Adam's breakneck driving.

The scenery slowly began to change and the land levelled out to gently-curving green slopes, where trees lined the road. A high wall followed the road on one side and it went on a considerable distance before Adam slowed down and stopped before huge, carved iron gates, supported by two white limestone pillars. He got out of his car and came over to Faye.

'You realise now it was the left turn you should've taken at the crossroads?' he said.

She smiled up at him. 'Yes, I do now. Mr Danby gave me the wrong instructions.'

'That's typical of old Danby. He doesn't know his left from his right. I'll open the gates for you.' He pushed the creaking gates wide open and waited until she drove through and stopped just inside.

'It's about a mile to the house. Great to have met you, Faye. Good luck in your new job. You'll need it where Luke is concerned.'

Faye thanked him and as she drove away, she watched through the mirror as he closed the gates. Adam, for some obscure reason had burst her bubble regarding her new post. When he had spoken of his brother there was animosity in his voice and she felt trepidation now at meeting Luke Montfort.

Lucy was mewing softly.

'There's no turning back now, Lucy. I've come to do a job and I'll see it through,' she muttered with determination in her tone.

The private road through Montfort land began to slowly ascend, but eventually the land levelled out again and became more cultivated. Several deer roamed the parkland, running swiftly away whenever the car was too near for their liking. Then Faye caught her first glimpse of Monkshill.

It was beautiful! Much larger than she'd imagined and built in black and white timber. At one end was a brick wing which must have been added much later. As she neared the house, to the left she could see what must be the abbey ruins, parts of it still standing intact, giving echoes of the time when it must have been a beautiful testament to the faith of those who built it.

She reached the house and got out of the car. The main door was of ancient dark oak, with a knocker in the shape of a lion's head in solid brass. Faye grasped the cold metal and rapped three times, allowing time in between. No-one came to the door, so she decided to look for another entrance. She had just turned the corner to walk by the side of the house, when a huge chocolate-brown dog suddenly appeared from nowhere and bounded towards her. It barked ferociously, but didn't try to attack her. She became rooted to the spot, terrified. She was wondering how to escape from her predicament when to her relief a man came from the rear of the house, whistling loudly to the dog, which turned and ran to him.

'There's no need to be afraid,' he

called. 'Darwin's bark is fierce, but he wouldn't attack you.' He patted the dog's head as he walked towards her.

'He did rather terrify me.' She held out her hand. 'I'm Faye Weston. I couldn't get anyone to answer at the main door.'

'You must forgive me, Miss Weston. My housekeeper has the day off. I'm Luke Montfort.' The hand which enveloped Faye's had a grip as strong as iron, despite the fact she noticed the swollen joints of his fingers.

'Shall we make our way into the house. I'm sure you must be tired and hungry.'

He led the way to the main entrance and they entered a large square hall. Several portraits of people in various modes of fashion lined the walls, whom Faye assumed were long dead Montforts.

'We'll go into the library. The sitting-room is rarely used. Faces north, I'm afraid. Would you like a sandwich with your tea, Miss Weston?' he asked,

12

opening a door indicating she precede him.

'Not if it is any trouble. I can always make myself something later.'

'I assure you, it's no trouble. May I call you Faye? I won't be long, make yourself comfortable.' He indicated she take a chair by the blazing log fire.

After he'd gone, Faye took stock of her surroundings. The room oozed masculinity. The soft leather armchairs were large and deep and held a faint aroma of cigars. There wasn't an ornament in any shape or form, only a photograph of an elderly couple sat on a desk that held a computer and was littered with manuscripts. Faye's gaze went to the patio doors which led on to a terrace, beyond which were neat lawns and farther still a dense wooded area.

Somewhere in the distance an almighty crash broke the silence. Darwin, stretched lazily on the hearth rug, jumped to his feet and padded to the door. Faye opened the door and followed the dog along a flagged stone passage to a door at the far end. She discovered it was the kitchen.

Luke was busy, trying to sweep up the shattered fragments of crockery from the floor with a pan and brush. Sandwiches were littered all over the floor. Darwin began to smell them with interest until Luke gave an order which the dog immediately obeyed and moved away.

'Please let me help you!' Faye said.

Luke halted in clearing the mess to stare up at her. His grey eyes held a hint of steel in their depths. His hair was raven black with touches of silver at his temples. Faye's gaze went to the fine lips, set in a firm line and she met his stare, colouring when she realised she had been staring too intently. His eyes narrowed as he returned her gaze without speaking for a brief moment. At last he spoke.

'Very well, Faye. I'll indulge you as it's your first day here, but I'm not in the habit of being pandered to. Mrs

Briggs, the housekeeper, is always trying to mother me since my wife died. I don't allow such nonsense.' He straightened and handed her the pan and brush. 'I don't know what happened. I think I turned and my sleeve caught the plate of sandwiches.'

Faye had an inkling Luke had dropped the plate, but she realised he must be embarrassed by the incident, so she asked in a cheerful tone, 'Would you mind if I made the sandwiches? I've brought some food from home with me. We can eat that.'

She went to the sink to wash her hands after clearing the mess.

Luke frowned. 'You may make the sandwiches, but we are not in Outer Mongolia. There is plenty of food in the cupboards and the fridge-freezer. By the way, you will take your evening meal with me in this part of the house daily. Did Mr Danby mention that?'

'No, he didn't mention it, but I would rather provide for myself. I understand there is a small kitchen attached to my apartment?'

Luke gave a faint sigh. 'Yes, there is, but I do hope you are not going to be awkward about it. While here you will be treated as an equal and it is my wish you dine with me in the evenings.'

'Oh, I certainly would not want to be awkward, Mr Montfort,' she spluttered.

'Please call me Luke.'

'It's just that I don't want to start off on the wrong footing. I mean you are already offering a decent salary and it seems over-generous to provide food also.'

'Let me worry about my over-generosity,' he said, a half smile on his lips. 'I'll show you where everything is, then perhaps we can get on and have our tea.'

He pointed to the large Welsh dresser, stacked with crockery and while Faye made the tea, Luke took some cans from a cupboard.

'There is ham or chicken, whichever you prefer. I'm easy to please. The bread is in that white container over

16

there. I'll leave you to it, if you don't mind.' He went out, with Darwin following at his heels.

Faye exhaled her breath. For some reason she felt this first meeting with Luke Montfort hadn't gone as smoothly as she'd hoped. He lacked the carefree attitude of his brother. His air of cynicism intrigued her enough to want to find out what had caused it.

2

When Faye returned to the library, Luke was standing near the window, staring out at a sudden heavy shower of hail. He turned and indicated she set the tray on the coffee table.

'I do apologise, I'm not much of a host, am I? Leaving you to do all the work as soon as you arrive.'

'Think nothing of it, after all that's why I've come here, to work.'

She smiled, earning a quizzical glance from Luke. She poured the tea into the china cups and handed one to him.

'Tell me, Faye, what was your first impression of Monkshill?'

'I thought it was breathtakingly beautiful and much larger than I'd imagined.' Her deep blue eyes shone with the memory.

'You're not the first to be bowled over at the sight of Monkshill. An ancestor of mine, Sir Piers Montfort, saw Monkshill and bought it immediately. It was he who was responsible for building the west wing in 1660, where your apartment is situated. I hope you'll be comfortable there.'

As Luke spoke about his home, Faye noticed how his features altered, making him appear younger than her first impression of him. She judged him to be around thirty-five and he appeared to be a quieter, less extrovert person than his older brother. Faye began to think he was not as forbidding as Adam had made out.

'I understand you had to give up full-time employment to care for your ill mother? That must have been a very difficult time for you.'

There was genuine sympathy in his voice.

'It was what I chose to do out of love, and I have no regrets,' she stated quietly.

'I believe you owned a tea-room near Hull. How long did you run it?' Luke asked.

'It was actually in Beverley, eight miles from Hull. Two years and I loved every minute of it. There are many tourists who visit Beverley as it's historic and has a beautiful minster.'

'Yes, it has. I've been to Beverley and know it quite well,' he replied. 'There are some very good tea-shops and restaurants there.'

Faye was taking a bite of her sandwich, which gave her time to decide whether she should tell Luke the real reason why the business closed. She didn't want to air in public the fact the man she had intended to marry, and who was in partnership with her, had left her for another woman. She was the one who had put up the capital to start the business and she'd foolishly put the money into a joint account at the bank.

Everything went well for almost two years. Custom was good, they were earning enough to save for their marriage, then Tony disappeared as if the ground had swallowed him up and the money in the bank account went with him. She heard from him six months later. He was sorry he'd walked out on her and taken the money. He'd met someone else and needed the money to start up again. He promised to repay her when he could, but nearly two and a half years later, she'd not received a penny from Tony.

She began legal proceedings and her solicitor was confident she would eventually receive the amount owing to her. She decided not to reveal any of this to Luke at this time, as even now her feelings for Tony were still bitter at his betrayal.

'My mother needed round-the-clock care for two years before she died. I wanted to nurse her at home even though it was both physically and mentally draining.'

He sent her an admiring glance. 'You are to be applauded. There are not many who would do that, not even for loved ones.'

Faye felt her cheeks burn at his warm

approval of her dedication. She was thankful when Darwin came to her and shoved his nose into her lap.

'He isn't at all as fierce as I first thought. Is he the only dog you own?' she added casually as she stroked Darwin's head.

'I don't need another dog where Darwin is concerned. He is a very good guard dog, but once he gets to know you, as I see he is doing already, he will be your devoted slave.' Luke gazed with fondness at his dog.

'I expect you need several cats to keep the mice away in an old house like this?'

Luke frowned. 'No, I can't stand them! I'd rather have mice around the place!' he said with vehemence.

Faye's heart sank. 'Cats are just as loyal as dogs. They are wonderful companions, once you understand their ways,' she said, determined to stand up in defence of her love of cats.

To her surprise he smiled. 'Like women I suppose, beautiful to look at, but crafty and cunning inside.'

'Are you talking about me again?' The voice from the doorway was soft with a seductive drawl.

Faye turned to see a woman, a few years younger than herself, entering the room. She was attractive in a sophisticated way with heavily made-up features. Her hair was a fiery copper colour and she had a pale flawless skin and green cat-like eyes. Faye felt a pang of envy at her slim, lithe figure in the black sateen leggings, which showed her curves to advantage.

'How are you, my darling?' She crossed the room and threw her arms around Luke, planting a kiss fully on his mouth. 'It's nice to have a break, but I'm always happy to return to the monks' playground.'

She turned her cool gaze to Faye.

Luke gave the woman a look of amused exasperation.

'This is Natalie Benson, my secretary. Take what she says with a pinch of salt. She is very irreverent about the monks who lived here centuries ago.' He turned to Natalie. 'Let me introduce my new tea-room manager, Faye Weston. She has only just arrived. I haven't even had time to show her to her apartment yet.'

Natalie's emerald eyes swept the length of Faye's body in an assessing manner. 'It's very isolated out here. I hope you don't get bored easily or are frightened by tales of spooks?' She gave a little laugh.

'I'll be too busy settling into my new job to be bored, and I'm not afraid of ghosts. You're not the first to warn me that the house is haunted.' Faye felt a definite hostility in the girl's reaction to her.

Luke shot her a puzzled look. 'Who has been telling you tales?'

'I took the wrong turning at Apple-wyke crossroads and I flagged someone down. It so happened it was your brother, Adam. He kindly came all the way back to lead me here.'

'Adam is always on the lookout for a

chance to practise his charm on some unsuspecting female,' Luke remarked in a sarcastic tone, making no effort to conceal his obvious dislike for his brother.

So it worked both ways with the brothers, Faye thought. Something must have happened to cause enmity in the family?

'Adam is the black sheep of the family, if you are not already aware, Faye.' Natalie gave a wide smile of relish, as if she was enjoying discussing the skeletons in the family closet.

'What else has my dear brother been saying about Monkshill?' Luke asked her.

'Nothing, he was very friendly and helpful. If it wasn't for him I would probably still be lost on the moors.'

Faye began to feel uncomfortable at the way Natalie had seated herself on the arm of Luke's chair and placed her arm around his shoulders. It appeared to her too intimate a gesture between employer and employee. Faye wondered if they were lovers.

'What made you apply for the tea-room post, Faye? Are you running away from something? A failed marriage or a love affair?' Natalie asked in her slow drawl, studying her red fingernails as she attempted to pry into Faye's private life.

Faye's cheeks turned red in a mixture of anger and embarrassment. It was Luke who came to her rescue.

'Faye has only just arrived and I'm sure she doesn't want to be questioned about her private life.'

Faye glanced gratefully at Luke. She didn't want to be rude by telling Natalie to mind her own business, but she did know she had taken a dislike to the girl.

'I'll help you unload your luggage from your car, Faye.' Luke stood up.

'Oh, I can manage. I'll bring them into the hall.' Faye felt panic rising within her. Now he would discover she had brought Lucy with her.

'You see how thoughtful your new tea-lady is?' Natalie joked mockingly.

'She doesn't want to trouble you too much.'

She sent Faye a sweet smile which didn't reach her eyes.

'If you would like to be unlocking your car, Faye, I'll be there in a minute to help you,' Luke insisted.

Lucy let out a distressed meow as Faye opened the car door.

'You poor thing. I'm sorry I had to leave you so long.'

She lifted her basket out and placed it on the ground. Her two large suitcases were out of the boot, when Luke emerged from the house. He approached her and frowned when he spotted the cat basket.

'You didn't mention you had any pets.' His tone was accusing.

'I haven't had the chance to. I was about to tell you I've brought my cat when we were interrupted by Natalie. If I'd known you have such an aversion to cats, I wouldn't have applied for the job!'

Luke stared hard at her. 'Mr Danby

must have thought you were the most suitable for the job and that is what is most important. As long as it stays in your apartment I have no objection to your keeping it.' He bent to pick up both her suitcases and she followed, feeling she'd scored a small victory.

Natalie was in the hall and her eyebrows lifted at the sight of Lucy.

'Well, you are honoured. It's definitely a first for Luke to allow a cat at Monkshill, well, since Helen died that is.'

'Dinner is at seven this evening, Natalie. Please be punctual,' Luke told her in a rather curt tone.

'Before you disappear upstairs with your new tea-lady, could I speak to you?' Natalie asked. Luke followed her into the library.

Faye turned away, feeling annoyed by the way Natalie referred to her as the tea-lady. She concentrated her attention on the various portraits around the hall. She was startled when her gaze went to one, which at first glance she took to be Adam or Luke, the likeness was astounding. She realised by the man's garb, it was painted either during the Civil War or a little later, judging by his long, flowing hair and tunic edged with a fine lace collar.

'That was Sir Grenville Montfort, a colonel in the Parliamentary army, another black sheep in the family, I'm afraid.'

Faye turned quickly to find Luke was standing just behind her.

'Your likeness to him is startling,' she remarked.

'Most of the Montfort men had black hair and grey or green eyes with the same sharp-angled features. A throw-back from our earlier Norman ancestors. Come, I'm sure you are more concerned about settling in your new home than my long-dead family.'

He picked up both her suitcases, bringing a protest from Faye.

'I'll carry one of those.'

'I'm not an invalid, you don't have to worry about me,' he said sternly.

Faye said no more and silently followed him up the wide oak staircase to the upper floor. They passed room after room and another smaller staircase. Whitewashed walls and oak beams in this part of the house gave evidence of its mediaeval origins, but as they walked on, the oak beams gave way to light, airy, decorated plastered ceilings. Faye guessed they had passed into the newer part of the house which Luke had informed her was renovated in 1770.

At last they reached Faye's apartment. Luke indicated to a door at the end of the landing.

'That door will lead you down the stairs into the herb garden. To reach the tea-room there is a path through the walled garden, but of course in bad weather you will need to use your car. The garages are integral now, in what were the cellars, so you won't have to go outside to reach your car. Before I forget, here are the keys you will need.'

He handed her a large bunch of keys and explained which were for the house, her apartment, the garage and the tea-room. He preceded her into the flat and stood aside as she entered the sitting-room. It was bright, modern and looked comfortable with a large sofa, armchairs, coffee table and in one corner the latest in wide-screen television and video.

Faye walked to the window and looked out on the herb garden Luke had mentioned. To one side she could clearly see the ruins of the old monastery, bathed in a golden glow from the setting sun. Following the shower everything looked fresh and bright green.

She followed Luke into the small, but well-fitted kitchen and was surprised when he opened the cupboard doors and saw they were filled with cans and packets of food. Then he moved to the fridge-freezer, which was equally bursting with frozen food.

'You'll not need to buy any provisions for quite some time, Faye. Mrs Briggs, the housekeeper, usually does her shopping in Fossbeck, the small market town five miles from here, but I have most of the household groceries delivered. Come through here, I'll show you the en-suite bedroom.'

The bedroom, like the sitting-room, looked over the garden. Her eyes strayed to the massive king-size bed.

'It's much too large for me,' she exclaimed.

Luke's expression was inscrutable. 'Mrs Lock, who ran the tea-room lived here with her husband, who did the gardening. After he died she stayed on for a while, but she was nearing sixty and decided to retire. Mr and Mrs Lock worked for my parents for fifteen years and they were very happy here. Now I have a gardener who comes in three times a week.'

'I hope I can run the café as successfully,' Faye murmured. 'I will do my best.'

'The bathroom is through here.' He opened a door and Faye was delighted with the pale lemon suite in a modern design.

Luke moved towards the door. 'I'll leave you now to settle in. Dinner is at seven. Just to welcome you and because I haven't any staff in today, I have ordered a catering firm to bring in our meal. Is that OK?'

'Oh, you shouldn't have bothered on my behalf!' Faye protested.

Luke's expression was enigmatic. 'It's no bother, I assure you. Meet me in the hall at six-thirty and I'll escort you around the house before dinner.'

After he had gone, Faye had a leisurely shower and did her unpacking. She didn't know whether Luke expected her to dress formally for the evening meal, but to be on the safe side she chose a velvet dress with three-quarter length sleeves and full skirt in midnight blue, which complimented her blonde hair and blue eyes.

Faye glanced at her watch. It was too early to meet Luke. She decided to put Lucy on her lead and find her way down the stairs to the herb garden. She put on her thick fleece jacket and zipped it up.

She opened the door at the end of

the landing and made her way down a flight of uncarpeted, stone stairs. The door at the bottom was locked and it took her several minutes to find the correct key. At last they were walking along a path, spilling over with plants of various kinds, which Faye recognised, chives, rosemary, mint, fennel and several more filling the air with their differing aromas. Lucy mewed with excitement at being out. She strained at the confining lead, but Faye daren't let her roam free, recalling Luke's request she be kept in the flat.

She came to an old iron gate where the walled garden was situated. She walked up the centre path to a fountain and stood for a few minutes admiring the carved gargoyles around the mouth of the fountain, then she walked on past the dozens of rose bushes, clipped down and awaiting their summer flowering.

She came to another gate and beyond were neat lawns, leading down to a lake. Faye guessed in summer it would be a lovely place to explore. She turned back and was nearing the iron gate which led back through the herb garden, when she heard voices nearby.

She peered cautiously through the gate, not wishing to eavesdrop on anyone's conversation. Faye could not make out what was being said, but she could see Luke and he was having what sounded to be a heated discussion with Natalie. His expression was dark with anger as the young woman berated him. She turned suddenly and walked away from him. Then all was silence. Faye wondered why Luke tolerated being spoken to in such a manner by an employee.

She was almost at the house when disaster happened. Lucy suddenly strained at the lead, which slipped through Faye's hand and the cat was away like lightning!

Faye sped after her around the side of the house and caught a glimpse of Lucy's tail disappearing under some bushes. She was obviously chasing something, whatever it was. She bent to peer under the bushes where she had last seen sight of her.

'What on earth are you doing, Faye?'

Faye straightened, her face red with embarrassment as she looked up and met Luke's bemused stare.

3

Faye scrambled to her feet with as much dignity as she could muster, with help from Luke's outstretched hand. 'I'm afraid my cat has escaped,' she said, breathless with the exertion of running. 'She saw a bird or something and ran after it into these bushes.'

Luke sighed in exasperation.

'I hope this is not going to become a habit?'

Faye's hackles rose. All this fuss over one small cat!

'Surely grounds as extensive as these can accommodate one cat without too much trouble!' she retorted.

At that moment, Lucy chose to emerge from the bushes. She walked sedately to Luke and brushed herself against his leg. He stared down at her, frowning. Before he could answer, Faye scooped the cat into her arms and marched away. Drat the man! If he insisted Lucy be locked up like a prisoner, she would leave Monkshill first thing in the morning!

True to his word, however, Luke met her in the hallway at six-thirty. He made no further mention of Lucy's escape and in fact was quite pleasant.

They began by going down to the converted garage which had originally been the cellars. Luke indicated which was the bay she would use for her own car. A ramp led up to double doors, which opened automatically by a sensor which was activated when the doors were approached.

Luke waited until she drove her car into the garage, then he led her up a flight of steps into the main part of the house and proceeded to take her on a guided tour.

'Several years ago we found it was no longer viable to keep the house purely for our private use. It's rather a headache, as you can imagine, trying to maintain a house as old as this without the capital to do it. We did think of letting the National Trust buy it. Adam was all for it, but my father wouldn't hear of it and stipulated in his will it must remain in the Montfort family.'

They were standing in a dark oak-panelled room. The huge four-poster bed was draped with ancient faded silk hangings. The sun was setting low in the sky, creating shadowy corners in the room. Faye felt a chill in the air which she hadn't elsewhere.

'This room is reputedly haunted by a monk,' Luke said, giving some credence to the cold atmosphere and acute depression she was experiencing since entering the room.

'Has anyone seen him?' she asked, feeling intrigued.

'Yes, my mother, many years ago, just after she was married. Apparently it only appears to women,' Luke said in an amused tone.

'Perhaps he was fond of women?' Her face fell. 'Oh, that didn't sound right!'

Luke laughed. 'Why not? It's a

well-known fact those professing holy lives did not always keep their vows. It's a true tale and rather a sad one. Dominic, the monk in question, lived at the abbey in the fourteenth century. He fell in love with Catherine, the daughter of one of my ancestors, when he came to the house to give the last rites to a relative of the family. They eloped together, but were pursued and caught. Tragically, Catherine starved herself to death to prevent her being forced to marry against her will. Dominic threw himself from the bell tower of the abbey.'

'They must have truly loved each other,' Faye murmured.

Luke's expression scanned her features with scepticism, his lightened mood of a moment ago gone. 'I doubt it. It was most probably pure lust because Dominic was forbidden to her.'

Faye glanced up in surprise at the contempt in his voice. He turned and led the way out of the room and down the stairs without further conversation.

His remark had set her thinking. Did he not believe in true love? Had he not loved Helen, his wife? As far as she was aware she had died from a terminal illness, or so Mr Danby had informed her. Surely Luke would have had some feelings for a wife going through such a traumatic time?

Dinner was something of an ordeal. It was Natalie's snide comments as they sat at table which ruined what would have been a pleasant evening.

The catering firm had provided a more than adequate meal of roast chicken fillets, salad, jacket potatoes and to follow, strawberry cheesecake and cheese and biscuits.

'Why on earth do you want to bury yourself out here on the moors, Faye?' Natalie's cat-like gaze slid to her. 'Especially when you are only managing the tea-room and not owning it!'

Faye almost gasped at her audacity.

'I could turn the question around and ask, why do you work at Monkshill when you could enjoy all the social life a city provides?'

Natalie's mouth tightened for a second, then she appeared to relax. 'Oh I've known the Montfort family for a long time, haven't I, Luke?' She looked to him for support. Luke, however, remained silent and non-committal.

'I'm almost one of the family,' Natalie continued. 'Luke's father was my godfather and our two families have been close friends for years. I'm just curious to know the reason why you applied for the job.'

There was an acid edge to Faye's voice when she answered. 'The plain reason is because I have to earn a living and I only know the catering business. I don't crave the bright lights of a city. I consider it a wonderful opportunity to be able to do the job I love in such beautiful surroundings.'

Luke came to her rescue. 'Faye doesn't need an interrogation about her private life, Natalie, as long as she does her job satisfactorily.'

Natalie pouted, but she didn't bait

Faye for the remainder of the meal. Luke kept the conversation going on various topics, including the history of Monkshill. Later they moved into the library to have coffee.

'The Old Friary doesn't reopen for another two weeks, so you will have plenty of time to settle in, Faye.' Luke's grey eyes swept over her.

She felt her pulse quicken at the admiration in his gaze, then she silently berated herself. This was the second time she'd allowed a Montfort brother to fill her head with romantic ideas. Why would he look at her when there was someone as beautiful as Natalie available? She suddenly realised he was speaking again.

'The tea-room is open from April to October, or earlier if Easter is in March and from ten-thirty in the morning until four o'clock every day, except Monday and Thursday when the grounds are closed. Mrs Lock used to help my housekeeper during the winter months when the tea-room isn't open. I hope you don't mind about that?'

Faye murmured she didn't mind at all and would help in any way she was needed.

'You'll find you have plenty of time to explore the moors, Faye,' Luke continued. 'If there is anything else you want to know, just ask. We all want you to settle down here and enjoy your job. Oh, by the way, breakfast is from eight o'clock onwards until nine.'

After that, Natalie began to talk to Luke about things which precluded Faye. She was thankful when the meal was over and she could excuse herself on the pretext of being tired. She said good-night and climbed the stairs, walking through the rather eerie corridors and landings to get to her apartment.

Faye slept well into the night until Lucy woke her, moving restlessly on the bed. She got up and went to the bathroom. When she returned to the bedroom, she realised Lucy's litter tray needed cleaning.

Faye ran her hand through her silky hair. She was fully awake now and it was only ten past four. She went to the window and drew back the curtain. Moonlight cast a silvery glow over the garden. She became aware of a light over near the abbey ruins and it wasn't moonlight.

It was a flashing light, like a very powerful torch. She watched for several minutes until the light faded altogether. Faye shivered and went back to bed. Who on earth would be out at this time of night, prowling around the old ruins? Luke hadn't mentioned having night security, but a house and grounds as extensive as this surely needed it.

She didn't mention what she had seen in the night and concentrated on the events of the coming day as she and Luke breakfasted alone. Of Natalie there was no sign. Mrs Briggs, the housekeeper, served them with a full English breakfast and Faye took an instant liking to Mrs Briggs, who immediately asked Faye to call her

Doris. She was a plump, homely woman in her late fifties with a blunt Yorkshire manner.

After breakfast, Faye was waiting in the hall for Luke, when Natalie sauntered by. She wished her good morning, but earned only a grunt from Natalie. Faye was glad she didn't have to work with the girl.

The Old Friary was a low, long building with a thatched roof. It had an old-world charm with dark green ivy clinging in thick clumps to the white-washed exterior walls. Luke unlocked the door and stood aside to allow Faye to enter first. The room was L-shaped with solid oak beams supporting the ceiling. The walls were emulsioned in magnolia and gave the room a cheerful appearance. The fireplace was of stone and in place of a grate there was a large black cauldron, filled with ferns and dried flowers.

Faye noted there were six round, oak tables each seating four. On each table were raffia place mats and small bowls in the shape of a swan for flowers.

'If you wish to alter anything, the fittings or décor, you are welcome to do so.'

Faye turned to find Luke staring rather intensely at her.

'I doubt if I will. It looks perfect as it is.'

He seemed pleased at her reply and moved to the counter and handed her a sample menu. 'This is our usual fare. You may wish to add to it. I'll leave that up to you.'

'I'll study it later,' she said. 'I usually do my own baking, quiches, sausage rolls and such like and I bake all the cakes.'

Luke eyed her with approval.

'Mrs Lock baked all the pastries and pies. Home-cooked food makes all the difference, don't you think?' His mouth curved into a very attractive smile and once again, Faye was reminded how very alike the Montfort brothers were in looks, but there, she realised the similarity ended.

There was a serving hatch on the wall behind him and a door to one side which led, presumably, to the kitchen.

'Come through to the kitchen. I think you'll find it clean and adequate.'

Luke was already moving in that direction.

She followed him into a bright, spacious, modern room, lined generously with white melamine cupboards. Here also the walls were magnolia with terracotta tiles on the floor. It was well equipped with a large fridge and separate freezer, microwave, dishwasher and a small gas boiler and water tank in a cupboard in one corner.

'I don't know if Mr Danby mentioned it, but there is a girl who comes in every day during the season to help you. Josie works full-time and when we are very busy in July and August, another girl, Karen, will help out. She has a young family and only does part-time,' Luke said, then he spent the next twenty minutes or so going through the procedures with Faye for stock ordering and the telephone numbers for the emergency services.

'Would you like to see the garden?' He unlocked the back door. 'This was Mr Lock's handiwork and he was especially proud of it.'

The garden sloped upwards and was built in terraces on three different levels. A path led up the centre to a pond with a water feature of a mill wheel turning the water continually. On one side of the garden, white patio tables and chairs were set on each level in small arbours, separated by trellis fences. Faye was pleasantly surprised to see several stone cats, discreetly placed around the garden.

'Oh, did Mr Lock like cats?' she asked.

A shadow crossed Luke's face. 'No, it was my wife who loved them.'

'Please forgive me. I didn't mean to bring sad memories to mind,' she murmured.

'There's no need to apologise. You were not to know.' He turned away abruptly.

Faye realised she must have stirred up painful memories.

'I've time to take you around the ruins before my business meeting in Fossbeck at eleven,' he said in a crisp tone, glancing at his watch. He began to make his way back down the path, then turned and looked at her feet. 'I'm glad to see you've a sensible pair of shoes on. Natalie will insist on wearing those high-heeled clumpy things.'

As they neared the ruins, Faye noted in places the abbey was largely intact. Much of the cloisters remained and the high altar and walls. In the bright morning light with the sun streaming through the gaps in the walls and the call of a curlew, the atmosphere was of tranquil peace. She could well imagine the monks in those long-ago days living out their holy lives in such a beautiful setting.

She remembered the lights she had seen during the night. Someone had been prowling among these stones. What had been their purpose? She was about to ask Luke if he hired night-time security, but never got the opportunity as at that moment she stumbled over a piece of stonework. Luke caught her before she fell.

'Have you hurt yourself?' He held her tightly for a moment.

'I should be more careful where I walk. I was looking up admiring the ruins,' she said, breathlessly. It wasn't the shock of nearly falling which had sent her pulses racing, but the feel of Luke's arms around her waist. 'It hurts a little, but I don't think there's much damage done.' She tested her foot on the ground.

They walked slowly back to the house, with Luke insisting she hold on to his arm for support. This made her feel even more uncomfortable. When they entered the house, he escorted her up the stairs to her flat and helped her to sit on the settee.

'Don't move until I return,' he ordered. When he did return he was armed with liniment and crepe bandages. He didn't bat an eye as he gently rubbed the soothing ointment into her ankle and bound it tightly with the bandages with amazing dexterity for someone disabled.

'If it's no better tomorrow, I'll take you into Fossbeck to see the doctor.'

'I'm sure it will be fine,' she replied.

'Make sure you rest it as much as possible, for today at least.' He moved to the door. 'If you want me to help you down the stairs for mealtimes, ring six-one-six, the internal extension in the hallway. Someone will hear it ring. Or stay here and Doris will bring your meal up.'

'Oh, I'm sure there's no need. I can take it slowly down the stairs.'

Luke's expression told her he didn't quite agree with her. 'If you're quite sure? By the way, there is a computer in Natalie's office. It's online and to save you having to drive into Fossbeck you can order all your food stock.'

'Very well. I'll look at the menu and later, when I've had a rest, I'll ask

Natalie if she doesn't mind my using her office.'

Luke frowned. 'No, of course she won't mind. You are perfectly entitled to use the computer. Let me know if you encounter any problems.'

He seemed confident there would be no problems with Natalie. Faye wasn't so sure and she was proved correct when, later, she hobbled down the stairs and entered the small office off the hallway, she encountered Natalie's disapproving glare.

Faye explained how she was going to list all the stock she needed on the computer and order online if she needed anything.

'Why should you need to do that?' Natalie asked in a sharp tone. 'Mrs Lock never bothered with a computer. Her husband used to run her into Fossbeck.'

'Apparently, Mrs Lock couldn't use a computer. Luke has made it clear it is what he wishes me to do.'

Natalie's expression darkened.

'You appear to have integrated yourself very quickly in this household. I have to use the computer constantly. I can't have you messing about and destroying my work,' she said in a supercilious tone.

'Let's get one thing straight, Natalie. I know how to use a computer as much as you do. I'm sure we can come to some arrangement when the computer would be free for me to use. If you have a problem about that, I think you'd better have a word with Luke.'

She turned and walked out, not giving Natalie the chance to complain further. If the girl resented her for some reason, that was her problem.

Apart from Natalie's unfriendliness, Faye began to settle at Monkshill over the next two weeks. Her ankle healed quickly and everyone made her feel welcome from Luke down to the two cleaners, who came in daily, everyone, of course, except Natalie, but she grudgingly allowed Faye access to the computer and there was a kind of stilted truce between them.

Josie popped into the tea-room the day before it was due to open, to meet Faye. She seemed a friendly, bubbly girl in her twenties and Faye felt they would work well together.

It was a beautiful day for early April. The sun was shining in an azure blue sky and the path along which Faye walked to the Old Friary was lined by a yellow mass of daffodils, swaying in the breeze on a carpet of emerald green grass. In the distance she could see Tom, the gardener, busy near the greenhouse. At that moment she heard a faint tinkling noise. Faye didn't take much notice, thinking it must be Tom, breaking something.

She drew in lungfulls of the exhilarating moorland air, feeling a new contentment after the traumas of the last few years. She approached the building and stood for a moment, letting her gaze roam over the picturesque view of the tea-room against the backdrop of trees and hills.

Her pleasure at the scene suddenly fell away from her like a cloak. Her eyes centred on one of the windows and she gasped in horror. There was a jagged, gaping hole in the pane. She ran the remaining distance and stared through into the seating area. Her horrified gaze saw the reason for the destruction. In the middle of the floor, where it had been hurled, was a large piece of rock. Someone must have thrown it deliberately!

4

Faye's hand trembled as she searched in her bag for her mobile phone. She rang Luke's mobile number, as she knew he had set off for Whitby just before she left the house.

'Don't worry, Faye, just keep calm,' Luke tried to reassure her when he answered the call.

'Call the police and I'll contact a glazier I know. I'll get back to you in a few minutes.'

At that moment, Josie arrived. 'Oh my giddy aunt!' she exclaimed, staring at the glass-strewn floor. 'Who would do such a thing and what for?'

Faye shook her head in bewilderment, as they went into the kitchen to make a pot of strong tea. She rang the police, but they said as it wasn't an emergency they might be some time getting to them. She explained she had to open the tea-room at half past ten, so could she clear up before an officer would arrive? The constable at the other end told her to put the weapon used to smash the window to one side, but not to touch it with her hands as it would be checked for fingerprints.

A minute later, Luke rang. 'Have you phoned the police?' he asked.

Faye related what they had said.

'That's typical,' he moaned. 'Well, you can't wait all day for them to arrive. Carry on with what you were going to do. The glazier, Tom Benson, will be with you in about an hour. I can't see any reason once the window is replaced and everything tidied why you can't open as normal.'

By the time Tom Benson arrived, Faye and Josie had swept up the shattered glass fragments and tidied the eating area. Faye put on disposable gloves and took the offensive piece of rock into the kitchen.

They were preparing the salad when Tom popped his head round the door.

'I could do with a mug of that tea before I start,' he said, eyeing the teapot. Faye and Josie smiled at each other. When Tom was armed with his mug of hot tea and a sausage roll, he went through to start replacing the window. It was now nine-fifteen. The quiches were going into the oven, and Faye began making the scone mix, while Josie put some rice on to boil for the salad.

Just before eleven, the new window was installed and the friary ready to open. The police had still not shown, but what could they do? It was an act of vandalism and too unimportant to waste their time. Half an hour later the visitors, who had toured the house and abbey ruins, were beginning to filter into the tea-room. An elderly American couple were the first customers.

They ordered coffee and scones, loudly enthusiastic about England in general and the Yorkshire Moors. It amazed them how far back the historic culture of Britain went.

'We think anything two hundred years old is ancient!' the bleached-blonde lady drawled. 'But you guys go back thousands of years!' Her mouth widened in a beaming smile. 'Oh, and these are just divinel What are they?' She took a large bite into the still warm scone, dripping with butter and laden with jam and cream.

'We call them scones here, but when you have them with jam and cream as you are, we call it having a cream tea,' Faye replied, smiling at the woman's enthusiasm.

'Oh, how quaint,' the woman gushed.

Her husband sat quiet, smiling broadly and taking it all in.

After that, she and Josie had no time to stand and talk. There was a steady rush with customers coming in and Faye was able to push the nasty incident of the smashed window to the back of her mind. It was nearly two o'clock before the police arrived. One lone officer, he asked if they had any idea who might have done it? Did anyone bear a grudge for some reason? Faye explained she had just taken over the management of the tea-room. The officer said they would get the piece of rock checked for fingerprints, but it was likely they wouldn't catch the person who had done it.

'Unless someone was hurt in the attack, the matter will probably go no further,' he explained.

'I don't think we can bank on the police to be of any help,' Josie remarked as they cleared away after their last customer.

'Yes, you're right. Unless it happens again, I think we should just forget it,' Faye replied. 'We've had a good day, customer-wise and I'm not going to allow some little hooligan to mar my pleasure in my new job.'

It was getting near to closing time, so Faye suggested they clear up and leave a little earlier. Despite the bad start the day's takings were quite substantial.

When she reached the house she tapped on the library door and at

Luke's call to go in, she found him working on his computer. Natalie was stretched out on the settee. She didn't know if it was her imagination, but to Faye there was a cat-that-got-the-cream, smug look on the girl's face.

'Not a very auspicious start to the day and the new job, was it?' she drawled.

Faye chose to ignore her mocking taunt. She was becoming accustomed to the malice directed to her from the girl.

'Do sit down, Faye. It's been a bit of an eventful first day, eh?'

Luke smiled, his sea-grey eyes taking in her tired features.

'You can say that again,' she remarked in a rueful tone.

'Would you like a drink? Sherry? Gin and tonic? Vodka? I think you deserve one.'

She stated her preference and Luke handed it to her before seating himself in the armchair opposite.

'Now this has happened I think it

safer if I collect the day's takings just before you close each day. Not that I don't trust you, Faye, but it's not wise to leave money in the shop safe overnight.'

'That's fine by me, Luke. I did feel uneasy about leaving it on the premises.'

'I'm sorry I was delayed in Whitby. I fully intended returning early this afternoon to help in any way I could.'

'There was very little you could have done, Luke. Once the glazier came and replaced the window, we tidied up and got on with the baking before we opened at eleven. The police took the stone, which was used to smash the window, in the event there are fingerprints on it. I'm just puzzled as to who would do such mindless violence? Has this ever happened before?' she asked.

'No, we are very isolated out here on the moor and besides there is nothing to gain, unless . . . ' He stopped speaking for a moment before continuing. 'Unless someone was intent on breaking in and was disturbed. Did you hear anything on your way there? You walked, I understand?'

Faye thought for a moment.

'Now you come to mention it, I did hear the faint sound of glass breaking. Tom was working near the greenhouse and I thought it was him.'

Luke's eyebrows drew together in thought.

'Tom wouldn't hear anything. He's quite deaf, but he won't wear his hearing-aid unless he is talking to someone. It annoys him too much. It could be the culprit saw you coming and had to leave pretty sharply.'

'I feel awful as it's my first day,' Faye said in an apologetic tone.

'Why should you feel like that? You are not to blame!' Luke said, his steel gaze scanning her flushed features.

'Perhaps someone has it in for you personally,' Natalie cut in.

'Nonsense!' Faye continued. 'Apart from the people who live and work at

Monkshill, I don't know anyone else in this area.'

'What about that woman, Josie?' Natalie persisted. 'She may resent the fact she wasn't offered the manager's job.'

Faye began to feel angry.

'You are making accusations without real facts.'

'Faye is right,' Luke agreed. 'Josie has worked at the Friary for two years. I offered her the manager's job when Mrs Lock retired, but she didn't want the responsibility. I suggest we forget the incident. It was probably only a one-off.'

Faye lay in bed that night, mulling over the conversation earlier that evening. If anyone was hostile towards her it was Natalie. Did she see her as some kind of threat? Surely Natalie did not view her as a rival for Luke's attentions? He was her boss and nothing more.

Then she recalled the feel of Luke's arms tightening around her waist when she had nearly fallen at the abbey ruins. Was she merely imagining there was more to it than the fact he was only ensuring her safety? One thing she was sure of, Natalie resented her presence at Monkshill.

The following days were uneventful. There was a steady stream of customers and Faye began to settle comfortably into the routine. Although they didn't have much time for idly standing around, if there was a quiet moment, she and Josie would snatch a quick drink and a sandwich and comment on the different customers coming into the Friary.

Faye was pleased the takings each day were substantial and she gave it to Luke when he arrived at the close of business to deposit in the safe in Natalie's office. Every week he drove into Fossbeck to deposit the money into the bank.

On one of her days off, Faye drove into Fossbeck to get to know the little market town and do a bit of shopping.

Being Thursday, there was no market that day, so Luke said the town would be quiet.

Fossbeck appeared to be a typical North Yorks town, several pubs, including a former coaching inn, a mediaeval church and a surprising variety of shops. Pleased with her purchases, Faye drove back at a leisurely pace over the moors. One day she was determined to seek out some of the strange places in this wild landscape, Mallyan Spout, a high waterfall, the Bridestones, Bronze Age standing stones, and the Hole of Horcum, a huge, natural hollow. It was such a beautiful part of Yorkshire and Faye wanted to see as much of it as she could in her free time.

She reached the entrance to Monkshill and was just about to turn her car off the road and through the gates, when she saw another vehicle sweep by on to the road. It was Adam's red sports scar, but he looked straight ahead and didn't acknowledge her.

'And a good day to you, too!' Faye

muttered to herself. He could not have failed to see her. Perhaps he'd had another tiff with Luke and was in an unsociable frame of mind. She put the incident from her mind until later, when she was speaking to Natalie. The girl was emerging from her office when Faye was on her way to the dining-room for the evening meal.

'I saw Adam leave Monkshill as I was about to drive in today,' she remarked; forcing herself to try to be pleasant to Natalie.

'You must have been mistaken. Adam hasn't been here today,' she replied curtly.

'Well, he may not have visited the house, but it was definitely him and his red sports car I saw.'

'If you say so!' Natalie said abruptly and walked off.

Faye didn't mention at dinner the fact she'd seen Adam. Luke seemed preoccupied and she had no wish to stir up Natalie's animosity again.

The following day was a busy one in

the tea-shop and Faye ran out of cakes by early afternoon. She realised she would have to bake more each day and made a mental note to add toasted sandwiches and teacakes to the menu, both of which appeared popular. They were clearing up in the late afternoon, after the last customer had left, when out of the window that looked on to the abbey, Faye saw a movement in the distance, among the ruins.

She realised it was Darwin and she waited for Luke to appear. Darwin wasn't allowed to roam at will around the grounds, especially so far from the house on his own. Just then the tea-room telephone rang. Josie was busy loading the dishwasher, so Faye answered it.

'Faye, love, Mr Luke has asked me to ring you.' Doris sounded flustered. 'He's got a visitor and he asked if you would put the money in the safe and lock the tea-room when you're ready to go home. He'll come later and get the money. Is that all clear to you? Also, Darwin went running off when I opened the kitchen door. Can you look for him on your way back to the house and try and get him to follow you?'

'Don't worry, Doris. I'll look for Darwin.' She rang off and when she and Josie had finished clearing up she said goodbye, locked the tea-room and began to walk towards the ruins, calling for the dog. Darwin suddenly appeared and bounded towards her, tail wagging and tongue lolling. He was a lovely, friendly dog and Faye had grown very fond of him, but now she berated him gently for running off from the house.

'You shouldn't be here on your own.'

Darwin eagerly lapped up the attention and the stroking Faye gave him and then he suddenly loped off in the direction of the abbey again, disappearing from view. She let out a sigh of exasperation. She would have to go after him and picking her way carefully over the uneven ground she spent a half hour looking for the dog to no avail.

'Oh, this is ridiculous, he could be

back at the house by now,' she muttered to herself.

Retracing her steps, she neared the abbey again and for a brief moment she forgot Darwin as she began to take notice of the beauty all around her. The tall, arched wall where the high altar had been looked magnificent against the backdrop of the darkening sky. Spots of rain touched Faye's face. She was wearing a fleece jacket, no protection in a heavy shower.

She walked on and left the ruins behind, into a part of the grounds she hadn't been before. It was thickly wooded here and as she scrambled through the undergrowth, she almost screamed when a deer ran across her path. She expelled her breath, her heart thumping loudly. Zipping up her jacket, she was glad she was wearing trousers to protect her legs as the rain was falling quite heavily now. The house was in view, but to Faye it seemed miles away.

A blood-curdling wail stopped her in her tracks. She was certain it wasn't a dog, they usually howled. She heard the sound again. Was it a woman, an animal? She moved forward, then suddenly her feet slipped from under her into nothing and she was rolling down a slope and thumping heavily on to her back at the bottom. The fall winded her and for several minutes she daren't move. There was a pain in her back and she gingerly felt over her arms and legs for any signs of a fracture.

But even as she lay there, getting soaked to the skin and in pain, the eerie, echoing wail registered in her mind. It was a cat, she was sure and it was very close!

She knew she had to move. The animal could be injured! Unmindful of her own predicament, she slowly rolled on to her side and levered herself into a sitting position. She glanced around and right in front of her was what looked like the opening to a cave. It had a sloping bracken roof, the one she had just fallen down. She pushed herself to her feet and limped over. She stared down and was surprised to see stone steps. She held on to the rusted hand-rail as she carefully began to descend, counting twelve steps, then she was at the bottom, standing on a stone floor. Facing her was an iron door.

It creaked loudly as she pushed it open. She was startled when a black and white ball of fluff shot past her up the steps. It was Lucy! When the little cat heard Faye's voice calling her, she stopped her mad dash for freedom at the top of the steps.

'How on earth have you got yourself trapped here?' Faye said, then the realisation hit her that she had left Lucy locked in the flat.

Someone must have been in her flat and Lucy had escaped. Another thought followed, more disturbing than the first. The door she had just pushed open had been closed tight! There was one thing she was sure of; there was no wind so it couldn't have blown shut by accident. Someone had deliberately brought Lucy down here and trapped her in.

5

She pushed the door wide open and in the dim light saw the walls were brick lined and the floor of stone. What was this place? It was cold with a dank smell and she couldn't imagine what it had been used for. She didn't think it was a tomb. There was a creepy feeling in the place, as though something bad had happened there, and Faye didn't want to spend another minute there, rain or not.

She gathered Lucy into her arms and was rewarded with a loud purr. She pushed her damp hair from her face and unzipping her jacket, she nestled Lucy inside then zipped it up again. The little cat rubbed her head gratefully against Faye's face.

'Come on, my pet, we'll soon be safe and warm in our flat and I'll get to the bottom of what's been going on!'

How could anyone do such a cruel thing to an animal, she thought as she trudged through the soaking undergrowth in the pouring rain. It could have been days before Lucy was found. She tried to dismiss the thought, it was too horrible to contemplate. Maybe some sick person did have a grudge against her, but to take it out on a defenceless animal was unforgivable. Faye felt the tears run down her cheeks to mingle with the raindrops.

The next moment a tall figure blocked her path. She jumped in shock and held Lucy even tighter in her arms.

'Faye! What on earth are you doing here?' Luke's anxious expression swept over her dripping hair and worried features. Darwin was standing by Luke's side, safely on his lead, but looking bedraggled. 'I came out looking for Darwin,' he said, taking off his rainmac and draping it over her shoulders. 'It appears to be a bit late for this as you're already soaked.' He held a large man's umbrella over them both.

'Come on, you need a brandy and some dry clothes.'

'Luke, wait a minute, please.' She stared up into his eyes. 'I was searching for Darwin and caught sight of him in the abbey ruins. I went after him, but he ran off. While I was looking for him I heard a terrible wailing noise and I found Lucy in a dreadful place, something like a crypt, back there. She'd been trapped in there and the door was closed.'

A frown creased Luke's forehead. 'That crypt, as you call it, was the old ice-house. It was built in Victorian times to keep the large blocks of ice needed to preserve food. Lucy could have merely wandered down there and the door blew closed in the draught. No-one would take her down there deliberately.'

'The door wasn't merely closed as you put it, Luke, it was shut tight. The latch was down from the outside. That's not the only thing. Someone has been in my flat. I left Lucy in there while I was at work. Who else has a key to my flat?'

'No-one now. Doris used to hold one when she was friendly with Mr and Mrs Lock, she used to look after the flat when they went on holiday, but she gave me the key when Mrs Lock retired. No-one else has a key, I'm sure. I didn't give the cleaners a key as you insisted you wanted to clean the flat yourself.'

'Well, someone must have. I'm very annoyed about this, Luke. I do expect to have privacy in my own apartment and why should anyone do such a terrible thing to my cat? I won't stay here if I think someone is intent on harming her.'

Luke glanced down at Lucy, squinting up at him through half-closed eyes. 'Helen was like you. If anyone had hurt her cats, she would have scratched their eyes out. Let's get out of this rain and we'll discuss it back at the house.'

He placed his arm around Faye's shoulder and held the umbrella over them as they walked silently back. She felt depression settle over her like the dark clouds above them. Coming to Monkshill, she believed, was going to be a new start for her after Tony's betrayal and then the stress of her mother's illness. Now it was all crumbling after only three weeks and she felt miserable and ready to give in. To add to all that, Luke had dismissed the incident, saying it was her imagination. Perhaps it was, she thought dejectedly.

When they reached the house, she moved towards the stairs, but Luke took hold of her arm.

'Don't let all this worry you, Faye. We'll sort something out. Natalie is going out for the evening. We can discuss all this tonight at dinner, alone.'

She wanted to take his advice and shrug it all off, but after the episode of the broken window and now Lucy she couldn't help but feel concerned.

Later, after having a shower and a hot drink with brandy added to warm her up, Faye began to rake through her wardrobe to find something to wear for the evening. In the end she chose a calf-length skirt in black velour and a figure-hugging emerald cotton sweater. The face in the mirror that stared back at her while she was brushing her hair was pale with anxiety.

The vicar at her mother's funeral had told Faye he believed her mother had been a strong person with the will to survive the many hardships in her life and that she, Faye, was in the same mould as her mother, but was she? She could give up and go back to Hull or stay and not be scared off by these events.

She turned from contemplation of her reflection and moved to the bed, where Lucy was curled up, recovering after her frightening ordeal. Faye ran her hand over the satiny fur. Lucy opened her mouth and mewed plaintively.

'I hardly dare leave you alone now, my pet.' Faye spoke softly. 'What are we going to do? Despite our bad start, I like it here and I don't want to leave, but I wonder what may happen next?'

★ ★ ★

Luke was already in the dining-room when Faye entered. His cool assessing gaze swept over her with admiration. Now she was glad she had bothered with her appearance.

During the meal of salmon, potatoes and fresh vegetables, followed by chocolate sponge pudding, Luke kept up a conversation on various topics. It was later, when they moved to the library and were sitting by the fire, having a drink, Faye told him of her possible intention to give him her notice.

'I don't even feel secure in the flat anymore and I am very unhappy about leaving Lucy alone. I am aware that to you she is just a cat, but she means a lot to me.'

'I know, Faye,' Luke replied in a

sympathetic tone. 'The only solution to that is to change the lock to your flat. The only ones who will have a key will be you and myself. I promise to ring the locksmith first thing in the morning.'

He lowered his gaze to the rich deep colour of the brandy he swirled around his glass. For a minute neither spoke and the only sound in the warm, cosy room was of Darwin, snoring where he lay in front of the open fire. Faye wished it could always be like this with just Luke and herself, without Natalie there with her acid tongue.

'Could I ask you to consider first before you decide to leave, Faye? I'll do all I can to be vigilant and if I find out there is foul play, the person or persons will be severely punished by making it a police matter. If you do decide to leave, then I have to accept your notice, but you understand I couldn't let you go until I have a replacement. Josie couldn't manage on her own at the Friary.'

'I would be willing to stay until you find someone. In the meantime, I'll feel much happier when the lock is changed.'

'It'll be done as soon as I can arrange it. I'll have a word with Natalie and ask her if any of the cleaners have a key.'

Faye glanced at the carriage clock on the mantelpiece. It was only nine-thirty but she felt exhausted.

'I hope you don't mind, but I am rather tired. I think I'll turn in.'

'Of course, Faye. You've had an anxious time today. By the way, how is Lucy?'

She was halfway to the door and turned, surprised by his concern for her cat. 'Oh, she's fine now. Once I made a fuss of her and she was fed, she forgot her ordeal. You've never heard such an awful terrified wail as I heard when she was shut in that ice-house.'

'Good, I'm glad she's all right. I may not like cats, but I would never harm them or any animal come to that, so you can cross me off your list of suspects.' The devastating smile was there again.

'I never have suspected you, Luke. You're the last person in fact,' she said softly.

Luke stared at her, his expression inscrutable.

'See you in the morning, Faye. Try to sleep well.'

She did sleep well and awoke only once to hear the lone call of an owl somewhere near. Faye woke late and groaned when she looked at her small alarm clock. It was eight o'clock and Josie would be waiting for her to open up. Her depression had lifted and while she was showering she had time to evaluate what she should do.

She liked her job at the Friary and Josie was easy to get on with. She was beginning to love Monkshill and the surrounding area. Besides, what was there to go back to? She had an aunt in Hull and one or two friends, but the city was not that far away that she could not visit them once in a while. Monkshill definitely had more going for it. She would not be driven away.

Just then her mobile phone rang. It was Josie, waiting outside the tea-room. 'I'm not anywhere near ready, Josie. Why don't you come here and have a drink while I get ready?'

Faye was getting dressed when the doorbell rang.

'I'll make some tea while you're getting ready,' Josie said, as she breezed in bright and cheerful as usual.

'I'm sorry I'm late. I was exhausted after last evening's events. Luke is getting the lock to my flat changed, but I don't know when the locksmith will arrive.'

'I'm all ears. Whatever has been going on?'

Faye related what had happened to Lucy as she brushed her hair and applied some light make-up. Josie listened intently as she made the tea and toasted some bread for them both.

'What a cruel thing to do to Lucy!' Josie exclaimed.

They were sitting at the table, hurriedly eating their breakfast Lucy, sitting in the sun on the window sill, turned her head at the mention of her name and stared across at the two girls.

'They must have a sick mind to put her down there after what happened to Helen.'

'Helen? What has Helen got to do with the ice-house?' Faye asked.

'Don't you know? Helen's body was found at the bottom of the steps leading to the ice-house. She'd been missing for two days and they left it as an open verdict at the inquest, probably accidental death.'

'Mr Danby, the person who interviewed me, said Luke's wife had died from a terminal illness.'

Josie looked sceptical. 'I expect because there was quite a bit of scandal surrounding the event and Luke wanted it kept from public knowledge, although it was in the local papers at the time. Helen was having an affair with Adam. This was while the old man, Charles, was still alive. He lived by strict rules and expected

Luke and Adam to do the same. Adam had a huge bust up with his father and was written out of the will. That's why Luke is the sole beneficiary even though he's the youngest son.'

'I wondered why there was such animosity between Luke and Adam, and why he doesn't live at Monkshill,' Faye said thoughtfully.

'The old man ostracised Adam, and he and Helen went to live at the other side of Fossbeck, where Adam still lives.'

'But if Helen had left Monkshill to live with Adam, what was she doing near the ice-house?' Faye asked.

'Apparently she'd gone to speak to Luke that day. It's rumoured she wanted him back because he was the one with the wealth and status. She didn't imagine Adam would be cut out of the will like that, left penniless, so to speak. Doris heard Luke arguing with Helen, then she stormed out and went missing. She'd fractured her skull in the fall and died from a blood clot, the coroner said.'

'Was the argument between Helen and Luke because he wouldn't take her back?'

'Everyone presumes so. Luke has never revealed what the row was about, but after what she did, I don't blame him not wanting her.' Josie got up to take the crockery into the kitchen.

'Leave those,' Faye called. 'I'll do them later. I've got extra baking to do today. Luke asked me if I would make a birthday cake for Doris, who's sixty in a few days time.'

Faye's mind was a whirl of activity as she worked that morning. All this time she had been under the impression that Luke had been happy and in love with Helen, but in truth she had been unfaithful to him with his own brother! That accounted for Luke's bitter, cynical manner at times. There was still the mystery of what Helen was doing at the ice-house on the day she died. Had she really tumbled or been lured there by someone and then pushed down?

There were so many unanswered questions.

Monkshill was not the peaceful, idyllic spot she had first imagined. If Helen had been pushed to her death could the perpetrator be the same one who had smashed the Friary window and locked Lucy up? If so it was a chilling thought to think they could still be at large on the estate.

6

Luke rang later that morning and informed Faye the lock to her flat had been changed and he would bring her the new key after lunch. Faye felt more at ease now, knowing no-one could get in her flat.

When Luke did arrive at the tea-room, it was full and busy in the garden where the customers were enjoying the spring sunshine. His strategy of advertising the reopening of the Friary under new management in local magazines and newspapers and in the tourist office in Fossbeck was paying off.

He stood for a minute, watching Faye as she served customers, unaware of his scrutiny. She looked attractive in her black pencil-slim skirt and white T-shirt, covered with a tabard in a white and green check. Her blonde hair was tied back with a white ribbon and her features were relaxed as she conversed with customers. In fact it was the first time since coming to Monkshill he had seen her so animated.

She turned and her eyes met his. Something happened to her in that moment and it struck her like a thunderbolt that she loved Luke Montfort! She tried to keep her features normal and maintain her smile as he walked towards her and dropped the key into her hand.

'I hope that makes you feel more secure.' His gaze held her own.

'Yes, it does. Thank you very much, Luke.' She smiled up at him, her eyes wide and clear. 'Would you care for tea, coffee? A piece of cake? Ginger, Madeira or perhaps carrot?'

'Whoa, steady-on, temptress.' He laughed. 'Unfortunately I haven't time. I'm trying to complete my manuscript on the history of Monkshill and I would like to finish the last chapter today. I wouldn't say no to a slice of that chocolate cream cake if there is any left after you close.'

'I'll put a slice away especially for you,' she promised.

When Luke had gone, Josie gave Faye a knowing look.

'I heard you trying to lure him with promises of cake.' She winked. 'And what wouldn't he say no to, eh?' She walked away, laughing.

'Go on with you,' Faye replied. 'It would take more than a piece of chocolate cake to attract Luke Montfort.' It would take someone like Natalie Benson, she thought.

The following days passed uneventfully. Nothing of an unpleasant nature happened and Faye dismissed all thoughts of leaving Monkshill from her mind. On one of her days off she decided to have a day out in Scarborough. May had come in fine and warm and Faye drove over the moors at a leisurely pace, reaching the town around eleven.

She strolled along Sandside past the

amusements then chose a café and sat on the terrace at the back, looking out over the beach and harbour, the castle walls dominating the scene. She was enjoying coffee when to her amazement, she looked up to see Luke smiling down at her.

'May I join you, or is your expression one of consternation?'

She gathered herself together. 'No, of course not. Please join me. I just can't believe in the whole of Scarborough we've picked the same café.'

'You're justified in not believing it.' He laughed. 'I must confess I was about to get into my car when I saw you enter the café. I've been visiting a friend and was about to set off back home, but I could do with a coffee first.'

The waitress came out at that moment and Luke ordered his coffee.

'Have you had lunch yet?' Luke asked, after they had finished their coffee and were leaving the café.

'Not yet. I was about to do some shopping first,' she replied.

'Can it wait? How about a walk along North Bay promenade? We could park our cars as near to Peasholm as we can and walk along the beach if you like.'

Faye didn't hesitate. She was still stunned by the revelation she loved Luke and any time alone in his company was precious to her.

They parked their cars and strolled along the promenade and then part of the way on the beach. Down here there was a cool wind blowing off the sea and Faye drew her cream jacket closer together. The sky was pale blue with cotton wool clouds moving swiftly across and not blocking the sun too long.

'This is the first time I've walked along a beach since I was a child,' Luke remarked casually. 'Even when Helen and I . . . ' He stopped speaking, realising he was about to reveal more than he'd intended. 'Well, the thing was, Helen didn't like the beach, couldn't stand sand between her toes.'

'Not like me then,' Faye said,

cheerfully. She had removed her sandals and was paddling at the edge of the water. 'I love the sand and sea. There is such a sense of freedom removing your shoes and splashing your feet in the water.' She was watching the sea swirl around her ankles, then ebb away, taking the sand with it. She glanced up to find Luke staring intently at her.

'Helen was nothing like you, Faye,' he remarked, not elaborating further.

The intensity of his gaze disconcerted her and she was uncomfortably aware of the blush on her cheeks. She hoped he would believe it was the fresh wind blowing against her face.

They moved from the water's edge and up the beach. Faye's feet soon dried and she finished off wiping the sand away with a handkerchief.

They arrived at a pub, close to the beach, and decided to have their lunch there. The dining-room overlooked a shallow, meandering stream running by the building and it was pleasantly quiet, with only one or two other couples enjoying a meal. They both chose a ham salad, the sea air having made them quite hungry.

'Would you like a dessert to finish?' Luke asked.

'Oh, no, thank you. I'm trying to lose weight.' She laughed.

'I don't know why,' he observed, his silver gaze sweeping over her. 'You are fine as you are. A woman who's too thin is not attractive.'

She felt secretly pleased at his remark. Perhaps he was not attracted to Natalie after all. She was, after all, only twenty-one and he was thirty-five, only three years older than herself.

'Don't think I'm prying, Faye, and tell me to shut up if I am, but is there no-one you've left behind in Hull?'

'If by no-one you mean a boyfriend, no. That is I left him behind long ago.'

'I can hear a hint of bitterness. Did he hurt you, Faye?' he asked gently.

'Not in the physical sense, but yes, at the time I was very hurt.' She hesitated, unsure of how much to reveal. 'Tony left me for another woman.'

'Had you been seeing him for very long?'

'Long enough, two-and-a-half years. We were saving to get married, until he went off with someone else with no explanation.

She looked down at her wine glass. Although she no longer loved Tony, to dredge up all the memories was still painful.

'As far as I can tell, you were well rid of him!' Luke said with vehemence in his tone.

'That isn't all he did. Tony and I were in business together, the tea-room I spoke of in Beverley. Fortunately it was in my name. I was going to sign it over to him when we married, but thank goodness I didn't beforehand, because when he left me, he drew all the capital from our joint bank account.'

Luke swore. 'Did you get any of the money back?'

'My solicitor has been fighting for years now to get what I am entitled to, but you know how these legal things drag.'

Luke's expression was dark. 'When we get home, give me the name of your solicitor. I'll try and hurry this up.'

'That's very kind of you, but you don't have to bother on my behalf.' she protested.

'It's gone on long enough. Let's face it. This man has stolen from you! He should be hauled before a court of law.'

'I didn't bring any charges against him at the time. I know I should have done. I was so upset and what with my mother being ill.'

Tears formed in her eyes.

'I understand,' Luke said softly and covered her hand with his own. 'Come on, let's go. We'll talk again about this.'

They caught the miniature train back to Peasholm Park, then walked the short distance to their respective cars. Faye wanted to do some shopping so she said goodbye to Luke. After he had gone, she realised today was the first time she had unburdened herself on someone since all the dreadful events of Tony and then her mother. She felt glad it was Luke who she had told. Her spirits were lighter, as though a great weight had lifted from her. All in all it had been a wonderful day out.

Faye parked her car in the garage and was looking forward to putting her feet up. After leaving Luke, she'd spent a couple of hours trawling round the shops, but hadn't bought anything. As she passed through the hallway, Doris was on her way to the library, carrying a tray laden with sandwiches and cakes.

'Enjoy your day out, love?' She beamed at Faye.

'I've had a lovely day out, Doris, thank you. Oh, let me carry that for you,' she offered. Doris frowned.

'I might be sixty now, but I bet my muscles could out do yours any day!'

'I'm sure they could, Doris.' Faye laughed.

'Mr Luke has been telling me you had lunch together in Scarborough.' She winked naughtily.

'Yes, we walked to the end of North Bay, but I don't know why you're winking, Doris, it was nothing like that!'

'Oh, just a bit of grit in my eye.' Doris beamed with good humour.

At that moment, Natalie emerged from her office. Her scowl spoke volumes, but she made no comment to either of them and moved across the hall towards the library. Faye was about to climb the stairs when she noticed Luke striding into the hall.

'Would you care to join Natalie and myself for tea today, Faye? I understand you must be feeling tired, but I would like to discuss plans I have in mind for more fund raising.'

She didn't want to appear unsociable, but after walking around the shops, the last thing she wanted was to share tea with Natalie. Dinner every evening was enough to cope with the girl's sly remarks.

Natalie, as usual, was stretched out in an armchair, raking her long, red fingernails through her hair.

'Would you mind pouring, Faye?'

Luke indicated the tea tray. He was rubbing his fingers and grimacing. She realised he must be in pain. It was something he never complained about, but she knew he had many bad days.

'Of course not.'

She smiled and moved to pour the tea into china cups. She passed one to Natalie and then Luke before handing them the plate of sandwiches.

'You're used to waiting on people, aren't you, Faye?' Natalie observed with a flicker of distaste on her features.

'I've had plenty of practice,' Faye said curtly.

There was silence in the room for a short while as they ate their sandwiches. Then Luke made a sudden announcement.

'The annual classical concert which was scheduled for July has been brought forward to June the twenty-ninth. I'm sorry for putting this on you, Natalie, but the quintet have informed me their concert tour of America has been brought forward.' Luke turned his gaze to Faye.

'I expect you are wondering to what I'm referring? Every year for the past eight years we have held a concert in the abbey ruins where floodlights are set up. My father began them and I have followed on the tradition, so to speak. It has been a great success in past years.'

'It sounds wonderful,' Faye murmured. 'Will I be doing any catering that evening?'

'No, it would be too much. We erect a marquee and provide a running buffet from an outside catering firm after the concert. I could do with an extra pair of hands though as the numbers usually exceed three hundred. Just to serve drinks. Not everyone stays for the buffet. Josie, Karen and Doris help out and even Natalie when she feels like it.'

'I'll be pleased to help,' Faye offered. 'I love classical music.'

Natalie snorted derisively.

'Always the one to help out, aren't you, tea lady?'

'I would appreciate it if you were less critical to Faye,' Luke surprisingly spoke up.

Faye sent a glance of gratitude in his direction. She didn't notice the darts of malice coming from Natalie's eyes or it would have given her something else to ponder upon.

★　★　★

In the next few weeks, Luke was busy making the arrangements for the coming concert. Faye saw little of him, apart from at dinner in the evenings. He had not mentioned any more of contacting her solicitor and Faye presumed it had slipped his mind in all the preparations, until one day she received a letter informing her that her case had been taken over by another firm. The bill for their services up to that date was included. She gasped at the amount owing. This was dreadful for doing precisely nothing in two years. Faye went immediately to find Luke to inform him she was dropping the case altogether. She couldn't find money like that to carry on.

Luke was in the library on his computer.

'Is it an inconvenient time? I can come back later,' she offered.

Luke rose to his feet.

'No, you've come at the right time. I need a break. After so long on here, my hands start to ache rather badly. Would you like a a glass of wine?'

'A white wine, please. I'll pour it,' she said, moving towards the drinks cabinet.

'Are you trying to mother me?' he said, giving her a bemused stare.

'I would never do that. I'm only giving your hands a rest.' She smiled.

Luke returned her smile.

'Are you happy at Monkshill, Faye, after that blip at the beginning?'

'Yes, I am. Now things have settled down and no more has happened, I feel very contented. The question I should be asking is, are you satisfied with my being here? Do you approve of my management of the Friary?'

'I am more than happy, Faye. You're doing a good job and I think we can dispense with a three-month trial now. If you are happy to stay here, than so am I. Let's drink to your continuing stay at Monkshill.'

Luke invited her to sit in one of the armchairs. Darwin as usual was never far from his master's side and when he saw Faye seat herself, he uncurled his sleek body from the hearthrug and nuzzled his nose into her hands.

'I've just received a letter from my solicitors, Luke, informing me they have passed my case over to Watton & Morgan. My solicitors have also sent me a huge bill for their services so far. Am I to understand you have had a hand in transferring the case?'

'I do apologise. I should have informed you before now that my own solicitors were taking over your case.

I've had so much to do, rearranging the concert. Apparently your boyfriend . . . '

'Ex-boyfriend,' Faye cut in. 'Well, actually he was my fiancé.'

'Sorry, ex-fiancé, has changed his address and is unable to be tracked down at the moment. They'll find him. If my solicitors can't help you, then no-one can. They are the best in the business.'

'It doesn't surprise me to hear Tony has absconded. It is typical of what he would do,' Faye remarked with cynicism. 'To get back to our discussion of solicitors, I would have liked to have been consulted first.' She handed the solicitor's bill to Luke. 'How am I supposed to find the money to pay this and the charges Watton & Morgan will make?'

Luke read the letter, grim faced.

'I'll take care of this, after all I did offer to help you.'

'I can't allow you to do that!' Faye looked aghast.

'Why not? Don't you like the idea of

being beholden to me?' Mockery edged his tone.

'It's not just that. Forgive me for saying it, Luke, but it isn't your concern. There is no need to be involved.'

His gaze seemed to bore right through her.

'I'm making it my concern,' he replied in a determined tone.

'I don't want to appear ungrateful, but if you do this for me I will pay back every penny I owe you,' she promised.

'You do that,' he shot back.

7

Faye was unable to sleep and got up to make herself a hot drink. She returned to the living-room to find Lucy sitting on the windowsill staring out into the dark night. Faye went over to her. She could see now what had caught the little cat's attention — a red glow, coming from the area near the ruins! Something was on fire!

The concert was due to be performed the following evening and the stage and marquee were already in place. Forgetting her drink, she quickly donned a sweater and jeans, and picking up her mobile phone she let herself out of the flat.

The air was pungent with the acrid smell of burning as she hurried through the grounds. She rang Luke's mobile number and told him as calmly as she could to ring the fire brigade.

'What!' he exclaimed, now fully awake. 'The stage and the marquee are on fire?'

'Yes, Luke. I'm standing in the grounds now.' She heard the expletive before he rang off. It wasn't just the fire that now held Faye's shocked attention, but the two figures, clothed in monks' habits, hurrying from the scene. They suddenly became aware of her and turned in her direction.

Faye turned to run, the thudding of her heart in tune with the hammering in her ears as she tried to outrun her pursuers. She recoiled in horror when a hand snaked out and wrapped around her throat and brought her to a halt. She was pushed to the ground and held there, unable to turn her head.

'Who are you?' she croaked.

A foot in her back pressed harder until she cried out in pain.

'Who we are is not your concern!'

The voice was muffled, but definitely male.

'What are we going to do with her?

She'll spoil our plans!'

The second voice was female.

Faye managed to slowly twist her head and look up. The woman's sleeve had slipped back and she saw, in the glow from the fire, a watch or bracelet around her wrist. Faye tried to make out the pattern and thought it seemed familiar, but the woman caught Faye's head and pushed her face into the ground.

'Keep your head down,' she hissed, her voice like her companion's, muffled.

The sudden shout startled them all. It was Luke and profound relief flooded through Faye as her assailants disappeared and silently melted into the trees. Luke came running to her.

'Faye! Are you hurt?'

He turned her over gently and helped her to her feet, holding her close against the warmth of his body.

This was where she had longed to be and without conscious thought her arms drew him nearer. His lips touched her neck, then he suddenly drew away from her.

'I'm sorry,' he breathed heavily as though trying to control his emotions. 'I shouldn't have done that.'

'There is nothing to be sorry for,' she said, feeling acute disappointment.

Their gaze held for long moments, until Luke turned his eyes to the fire and the spell was broken.

'Have you called the fire brigade?' she gasped, trying to still her chaotic mind.

'Yes, they're on their way. I hadn't been asleep long when you rang. Did they hurt you?' he asked.

'No, I don't think so.' She was trembling violently with shock and Luke took off his jacket and wrapped it around her shoulders. 'What a terrible thing to happen when everything was ready for the concert.'

'I don't care about the concert,' he muttered. 'It's you I care about. Why on earth did you come out here in the dark alone?'

There was anger in his tone.

'I couldn't sleep. I looked out of the

window and saw the glow of the fire. I came out to investigate. Why would they want to ruin the concert, Luke?'

Before he could answer, they both had to quickly back away as the raging inferno which had been the marquee collapsed suddenly into a heap of burning embers. Luke's features in the flickering red light from the fire were drawn deep in thought.

'I have a pretty good idea who is behind all this and why,' he stated gloomily.

Faye wondered if Adam was under suspicion. She winced suddenly as pain wrenched her lower back, causing Luke to turn from his contemplation of the fire to stare at her with concern.

'You are in pain!' he exclaimed, seeing her face contort.

'One of them kept me pinned to the ground with their foot in my back.'

'Come on, you need a hot drink and some painkillers. There is nothing we can do here. By the time the fire engine arrives, the fire will have burned itself out!' He turned to look at the blazing shell which had been the stage.

They walked back in silence, each in their own thoughts. Faye tried to concentrate on Luke's statement that he had his suspicions who was the arsonist, but her mind kept focusing on when he had held her close in his arms and he had said, 'It's you I care about.' Was it just the employer in him speaking or had he meant something more deep and personal?

Luke sat her down at the kitchen table while he made the tea, and cheese sandwiches. Just then they heard the wail of the fire engine siren approaching. He hurried out to direct them to the fire.

Faye placed the tea and sandwiches on a tray and carried it into the library, followed closely by Darwin at her heels, hoping for a titbit.

Luke entered a few minutes later.

'I doubt they'll have much to douse,' he said ruefully.

He went to the tray and picked up a

sandwich and mug of tea.

'I'm so sorry, Luke. What an awful thing to happen when the concert is so near. I know just how much hard work you've put in over the last few weeks, organising it. How can people do such things?'

She shook her head in bewilderment.

'They can when they are eaten up with jealousy and the need to seek revenge!'

Faye was convinced now he was referring to Adam and the fact he'd been written out of their father's will.

'Have you taken any painkillers yet?'

When she shook her head he moved to his work desk and took a packet from a drawer. 'Take two of these for your back pain and if it's no better in the morning I'll make you an appointment to see the doctor.'

She took the tablets and swallowed two with her drink. 'Are you trying to mother me?' she asked, with a glint of humour in her voice.

'Touché,' he murmured, his usual

stern expression softening. 'I seem to recall accusing you of that. I've come to rely on you for so many things, Faye.' He moved nearer and placed his mug on the coffee table. She held her breath as he drew her into his arms and bent his head.

His lips touched her own, gently, then it was as though something inside them both exploded and Faye rose to meet the passion in his kiss. The noise of the door opening had them springing apart. Natalie sauntered in, stifling a yawn.

'What on earth is going on out there? The din is enough to waken the dead!' She pushed a hand through her tousled hair. She was wearing a cotton house-coat in blue satin, tied around the waist and her feet were bare.

'The concert stage and marquee have been destroyed by fire, Natalie,' Luke explained. His expression was dark with annoyance and Faye wondered if Natalie's interruption was as unwel-come to him as it was to her. Had

Natalie guessed they were kissing? She had made no sign if she had.

'Who would do that?' Her green eyes widened.

'I didn't say anyone had.' Luke stared at her thoughtfully. 'We have yet to find out.'

'Faye, be a darling and make me a coffee?' Natalie asked sweetly.

'Faye will do no such thing! You are quite capable of making your own drink!' Luke's tone was sharp.

'Don't be cross at me, just because your stupid stage has gone!' Natalie replied, flouncing out.

'Faye, may I ask you not to mention the hooded figures to Natalie?' he asked. 'I don't want this reported all over the moors to Fossbeck and beyond.'

'Of course not, Luke. Besides, I'm hardly Natalie's best friend!' she replied with a sigh.

A half smile curved his lips.

'So I've noticed. Faye, what happened just now between us, please accept my apology. I don't know what came over me.'

'There's no need for an apology, Luke. Let's forget it happened. I think we both must be tired.' She tried to stifle her rejection that was threatening to dissolve her composure. 'If you don't mind, I'll say good-night.'

She moved to the door.

'Good-night, Faye. I hope we'll both be able to sleep.' She turned to look at him. His features were grim, his mouth set in a tight line.

She made her way through the moonlit corridors and landings of the old house to her flat, her mind full of the night's events, not least Luke's passionate kiss and his instant regret it had happened.

Tears blurred her vision, then she saw a movement in front of her. The figure of a monk, several yards ahead, walked across her path. She stopped, her heart hammering with fear. Was it one of those who had chased her and some-how entered the house?

It disappeared from her sight. She slowly walked up to where she had seen the figure. There was nothing but the wall! No human can walk through solid walls! Faye suddenly realised it was no human she had seen, but the lovelorn ghost of Dominic. Her fear gone, she felt an overwhelming sadness. Now she knew what it felt like to be in love with someone she could never have.

She entered the flat and sank on to the bed, burying her face into her pillow. Tears flowed down her cheeks and at first she took no notice of the silky, furry head nuzzling her face. Faye reached out her hand and brought Lucy close, hugging the small body to her. The gentle purr soothed her misery. She had seen for herself the legendary ghost of Monkshill, but all she could think of in that moment was Luke's rejection of her!

She slept fitfully for the reminder of the night. It was Thursday, one of the days when the tea-room didn't open, planned to coincide with the day of the concert so that she could help with the evening's catering. Now the concert could not take place.

After breakfast, Faye decided to visit the ruins to see the damage in the light of day. She fitted the harness on Lucy and led her downstairs into the herb garden, walking slowly to give the little cat a chance to sniff at various spots along the way. The morning air was tinged with the smell of burning wood.

When she neared to where the concert was to have been held, she stood staring at the blackened remains of the stage and marquee. She shook her head at the wanton destruction! No wonder the people responsible had disguised themselves! She turned back and was almost at the house when she saw Natalie walking along the path towards her.

'Good morning, Natalie.' She greeted her as pleasantly as she could.

The greeting was ignored.

'Luke wishes to see you, now!' Natalie's voice was harsh with anger.

Faye bit her lip to prevent her answering the girl in the same hostile manner.

'Don't think I didn't notice you were simpering around Luke last night, trying to gain his sympathy and what else, I wonder?' Natalie said. 'You both seemed very guilty about something when I walked in.'

'Whatever it was isn't your business,' Faye retorted. 'Your imagination must have been working overtime, Natalie.'

She was determined not to let the girl's hostility get to her.

'Don't think Luke will ever look at you! He likes women younger, prettier and slimmer than you!'

Natalie swept by, but not before Faye caught a flash of the silver bracelet around her arm. Her malicious remarks were ignored as a cold hand gripped her heart.

She was sure the bracelet was the same one she had seen around the hooded woman's wrist the night before. It was careless of Natalie to wear it, unless she wasn't aware Faye had seen it. It couldn't be mistaken as it was an unusual design of watch and bracelet combined with the strap made up of tiny silver horses. Faye had often noticed it and secretly admired it.

She was in a dilemma. Should she tell Luke of her suspicions? Why would Natalie want to work against Luke and Monkshill? She had declared her closeness to the Montfort family and she was Luke's secretary. She had made it clear she wanted Luke for herself; her outburst just now confirmed it.

Her mind was a whirl of indecision as she made her way through the house, after leaving Lucy in the flat. She stopped briefly at the spot where she had seen the phantom hooded figure the night before. There was absolutely no way, if it had been human, that he could have gone that way, short of walking through a solid wall. Faye moved on as mystified as ever by all the strange events she had encountered since coming to this house.

Doris was emerging from the dining-room as Faye reached the hall.

''Morning, love. Would you like some breakfast? Mr Luke is eating his now. He got up late today.'

'I've had breakfast in my flat, thank you, Doris. I wouldn't say no to another cup of tea, if there is any?'

'I'm just going to make a fresh pot for Mr Luke. He's not very happy this morning about that to do last night.'

'Yes, I'm afraid the concert will be cancelled,' Faye murmured.

'I can't understand why folk do such nasty things.'

Doris moved away, muttering to herself.

When Faye entered the dining-room, Luke glanced up and smiled, but she couldn't help noticing the dark shadows under his eyes. 'How are you this morning? Has your back pain gone?' he asked, pleasantly.

Faye seated herself on the chair he had pulled out for her.

'Quite well, thank you, despite the

events of last night and then having seen Dominic after I left you, on my way to the flat.'

She spoke so casually, Luke raised his eyebrows over the rim of his cup, halting midway in taking a swallow of liquid.

'Dominic? You mean our legendary ghost? Are you sure?'

'As sure as one can be about the paranormal. He walked across my path, wearing a dark habit. For a moment I thought it was one of those ghastly people who we believed started the fire and that somehow they had entered the house, but the figure literally disappeared through the wall.'

Luke gave a low laugh.

'Can you remember where you were when you saw him?'

'Oh, yes.' Faye proceeded to tell him.

'Dominic was making his way to the haunted room,' Luke answered. 'It's just the other side of that wall. I don't think I related what happens to those privileged to see him, did I?'

Faye's smile faded. 'Oh, is it something dreadful?'

'No, quite the opposite. It is said you find your greatest happiness and never leave Monkshill.'

His gaze was intense and Faye looked down.

'I tend to regard such tales with a pinch of salt, I'm afraid.'

She was glad Doris chose that moment to bring in the tea tray.

'I wouldn't dismiss it so lightly if I were you,' he remarked in a serious tone. He glanced at his watch. 'We have to inform everyone today who bought a ticket that the concert is off for the foreseeable future. I've already rang the quintet leader. Natalie will have to do most of the notifying and arrange for the money to be refunded.' He gave a deep sigh. 'I could have done with that money now. The east wing has a hole in the roof and badly needs repairing. I'll try and organise the concert for later in the year, perhaps August. We have to determine yet whether it was arson.'

'I didn't actually see those hooded people start the fire,' Faye explained, pouring tea for them both. 'But they were acting very suspiciously. They obviously thought I was a threat to them.'

She stopped speaking, wondering if it was wise to reveal her suspicions to Luke. 'I don't know whether I should say anything, but it was something you said, about having a good idea who may be behind all this. My own suspicions were aroused last night, when those people caught me, but I wasn't sure, until this morning . . . '

Luke frowned. 'What are you trying to say? Tell me everything that happened.'

Faye took a deep breath.

'One of those figures was a woman. I couldn't recognise her voice because their hoods were over their mouths and muffling their voices. As they held me to the ground I managed to turn my head and I caught a glimpse of a bracelet around her wrist. I seemed to think it was familiar.'

There was a long silence when Faye halted. Luke's features had darkened. 'Carry on, Faye. If you have information that may be useful to the police they must be informed.'

'I saw the same bracelet this morning, on Natalie's wrist,' Faye stated quietly.

'What! No, you must be mistaken!' Luke ground out, his voice harsh. 'She wouldn't be involved in something against me and Monkshill!'

'Why wouldn't she?' Faye dared to ask.

His manner suddenly became cold and distant, as if an invisible barrier had dropped between them.

'I've known Natalie since she was born. She is totally loyal to me. I won't listen to such accusations! Many bracelets appear similar.'

'I can only tell you what I saw, Luke. Natalie's bracelet watch is very unusual. Why are you so convinced she couldn't be involved?'

'Because it's impossible for Natalie to

be capable of such action. I'm beginning to think you are accusing her from a sense of injustice against yourself!'

'What do you mean by that?' Now it was Faye's turn to be affronted.

Luke's steel gaze bore through her.

'I'm well aware you dislike Natalie. Are you jealous of her, Faye?'

She gasped. 'This conversation is becoming ridiculous! The dislike is not all on my part. I've gone out of my way to be pleasant to her and I am constantly rebuffed!' Her blue eyes spat darts of fire. 'As for jealousy, Natalie has nothing I covet!'

'I wonder,' he murmured half to himself. 'Until you can substantiate what you have said, I suggest you keep your suspicions to yourself!' His voice was icy.

Faye rose to her feet and left the room without another word. She had not expected Luke to wholly believe her, but his hostility had surprised her.

Tears sprang to her eyes. How could she prove she was not accusing Natalie out of a sense of revengeful spite?

126

8

Faye felt she needed time to think about her future in the light of last night's events and her conversation with Luke this morning. Once before she had considered leaving Monkshill, but now she felt her position was untenable with him viewing her as a person who threw wild accusations at a member of his staff from sheer jealousy. There was little option but to inform him of her intention to give one month's notice.

The previous night when the mask of employer had dropped and Luke had kissed her passionately as a man who desired her, her heart had soared with happiness, then the bubble had burst when he'd apologised and now in the cold light of day perhaps he was using Natalie as an excuse to warn her off.

She sighed. Perhaps it was better to

leave Monkshill and let the Montforts fight their own battles. From the start someone hadn't wanted her there and now she was certain it was Natalie. Well, she thought mutinously, she could have Luke all to herself. She was fed up with them both.

*　*　*

After she had closed the tea-room that afternoon, Faye drove into Fossbeck to buy some cat food and other items she needed and didn't arrive back until six o'clock.

After feeding Lucy, she had a shower then made herself a salad and didn't bother to get dressed again. So she felt somewhat embarrassed when there was a knock on her door at eight. Tying the sash of her cotton-towelling robe more tightly she went to answer it.

Luke stood there, casually dressed in jeans and a black cotton sweater. He looked darkly handsome and her heart beat quicker.

'May I come in or is it inconvenient?'

His eagle-eyed gaze took in her state of undress and hair newly shampooed, falling in shining soft waves around her face.

'No, come in, Luke. Please excuse my appearance, I've just showered. I went into Fossbeck after I closed the Friary.'

She stood aside to allow him to enter.

'So I gather,' he remarked dryly. 'Have you been avoiding me? You didn't come for dinner.' He moved into the centre of the room.

Lucy ran to him and rubbed against his leg. Luke stared down at her and to Faye's surprise he bent down and stroked the cat's soft fur.

'Would you care for a drink? Whisky? Brandy?' she asked.

'A whisky will be fine thank you, with soda.'

He sank into an armchair. Lucy immediately leaped on to the back of the armchair and sniffed the back of Luke's hair.

'Lucy!' Faye exclaimed. 'I am sorry, Luke. Shall I put her in the bedroom?'

'No, she's not doing any harm. You didn't answer my question,' he said, scrutinising her flushed features as she handed him the drink. 'Are you avoiding me?'

'Of course I'm not,' she answered, annoyed by his interrogation. 'I needed to clear my head and make a decision.'

'And have you?'

There was tension in his body as he waited for her answer.

'Yes,' she took a deep breath. 'I think it would be in all our best interests if I gave you my notice.'

Luke's gaze narrowed. 'I presume you came to this decision after our conversation this morning?'

'I hope you understand I cannot stay here now.'

He suddenly rose to his feet, his features dark with anger. 'All I understand is that you appear to be running away!' He moved towards her.

She gripped together the edges of her

robe under his eagle-eyed gaze.

'And if I am, can you blame me? I can't work for you knowing how you regard me.'

'How do I regard you, Faye?'

His gaze seemed to strip away her closely-guarded emotions, leaving her vulnerable where he was concerned. Having nothing to lose now she decided it was time for plain speaking.

'As a green-eyed monster, driven by my own inadequacies. As for avoiding you, yes, I was. Both you and Natalie. I don't know what motives she has for doing these things against you, but I will not be the butt of her vicious games!'

Luke's mouth curved in a grim smile at the darts of ice directed to him from her cold eyes.

'You are so sure it was her. Very well, I will give you the benefit of the doubt. I'll reserve my judgement of Natalie and you remain here. I don't want you to leave.' He turned away, his expression shielded from her view.

A surge of hope rose within her, but his next words totally destroyed her illusions.

'You are running the Old Friary very successfully and profits have gone up considerably since you came. I would be hard put to find anyone as good at the job as you.'

A heavy weight crushed all her dreams. All he cared about were his financial profits and nothing for her as a woman.

'Please say you'll stay, for the time being at least? The fire brigade rang me. It was arson. They found traces of petrol among the ashes. I want to get to the bottom of this as much as you do.'

Faye met his gaze which held a hint of pleading. She gave in, realising even though he didn't love her, she loved him and couldn't bear to be parted from him. Not yet anyway. She had to find proof that it was Natalie behind the arson attack and perhaps also the smashed window. Had she also shut Lucy in the ice-house? It could not be discounted if the girl was intent in making things as difficult as she could to force her to leave Monkshill.

'Very well, Luke, I'll stay for the time being. I will, however, not be dining with you in the evenings. I prefer to keep to myself from now on.'

'If that's what you prefer.' His expression lightened suddenly. 'I'm glad you've changed your mind about staying, Faye. We'll get this sorted out, don't worry.' He moved to the door, then turned, assessing her figure with an enigmatic expression. 'You look beautiful tonight.'

He was gone before she could answer. She went to gaze in the mirror at her reflection, hugging his last remark to herself. Beautiful was the last word she would attribute to herself, but Luke was not the kind of man to speak idly. She went to bed that night in a much happier frame of mind.

* ★ ★

Over the next few days, Faye barely saw Luke or Natalie as she had kept her intention not to have dinner with them in the evening. But sometimes in passing the dining-room she heard them laughing together and a streak of jealousy stabbed at her. She had isolated herself from their company and the feeling of being a social outcast was very unsettling.

One evening, Josie asked Faye if she would to go the cinema in Scarborough with her. Faye agreed, needing a break. They both enjoyed the romantic adventure film and afterwards went for a meal in a restaurant. By the time they had driven back across the moors in Faye's car and she had dropped Josie off at her home near Fossbeck it was nearing midnight.

Faye parked her car in the basement garage and was intending to go straight to bed. She had to be up at six as there was extra baking to do for the weekend visitors. Trade was picking up and the two most busy months of the year were almost on her.

She locked her car and was just about to walk to the flight of stairs which led up to the entrance to the hall when she heard someone enter the garage. Faye caught a glimpse of Natalie as she descended the stairs. She didn't want to verbally spar with her at this time of night, so she quickly squatted down beside her car, wondering where she was going at such a late hour.

Faye lifted her head to see her disappear into the storeroom. Several minutes ticked by, but as everything remained quiet, she began to wonder what the girl was doing in there. It was only a room where equipment and spares for the cars were kept.

She crept towards the storeroom and listened. There was total silence, so she cautiously opened the door. The room was empty and there was nowhere for Natalie to conceal herself.

Faye gazed round, mystified. Where on earth could she have gone? Then she noticed the dark crack in the wall. As she got nearer, Faye realised it wasn't a crack, but a door that had been left ajar. Opening it fully she could see only blackness beyond. Was it another room or a tunnel? She needed a torch and hurried back to the car for the large flashlight she always kept in the boot.

On her return she flashed the light into the darkness, revealing it was a tunnel, very narrow and about six feet in height. Luke had never mentioned the existence of such a construction, but Faye knew many ancient buildings had escape routes and secret rooms. What was Natalie up to now? Where did the tunnel lead? Faye felt some trepidation, but she knew she would have to do something if she was ever going to prove Natalie was not the innocent victim Luke believed her to be.

Armed with the torch, she stepped into the chill, musty tunnel, thankful she was wearing jeans and a thick sweater. Her mobile was clipped safely to her waistband.

The tunnel turned at various intervals as she walked on until she came to a halt. It divided into two separate paths! She was in a dilemma, not knowing which one to take. The sensible course would be to go back and ask Luke about the tunnel in the morning, but now she had come this far she had to find out where it led.

She decided on the right-hand path and tried as she walked to picture in her mind which direction she could have gone. It was impossible. There were so many twists and turns she could be in the middle of the moors for all she knew and for the last few minutes the path had graduated gently upwards.

At last she could go no farther. A wooden door barred her way. A gust of air blew in from a large crack in the door. She flashed her torch downwards and saw a large iron ring handle. She grasped the cold metal and turned it, pushing as she did so. The door was stiff, but she managed to open it wide enough to pass through. She was standing in the cloisters of the abbey.

The wind made a moaning sound as

it blew around the colonnades. The moonlight gave the stonework a pale ethereal appearance. She shivered. Was she mad, stalking around these ghostly ruins at midnight alone?

There was no sign of Natalie. Had she taken the other pathway in the tunnel, wherever that led? An owl screeched as it lunged to the ground in pursuit of its prey. Faye decided this was madness and began to walk as fast as she could through the cloisters, wishing she were tucked up in bed. She did not get far before a figure, clad in a dark habit, suddenly blocked her path. She jumped back, terrified by the tall, silent form crossing its arms like an avenging angel. Faye was prepared for flight when the figure reached up and pulled back its hood.

She gasped, immediately recognising the sharp angles of the man's features, so like Luke's.

'Adam! I might have guessed.'

Faye was not altogether surprised to see Luke's erring brother.

'Not surprised to see me, Faye? I wonder why.' His tone was mocking.

'I saw you drive away from Monkshill, several weeks ago when no-one else seemed to have seen you. I wondered why you had come then.'

A thin smile twisted Adam's rather cruel-shaped lips.

'Poking your nose in where you don't belong, eh?'

'From what I've heard, I belong here at Monkshill more than you do, Adam.' She tried to brave it out.

In the pale light from the moon, Faye watched his features contort into a mask of fury. 'Why, you little . . . What has Luke been telling you?'

'He has told me nothing of your family feud. I found out elsewhere. Are you responsible for the fire and the broken window of my tea-room?'

'No, I didn't smash your window. Natalie has that dubious honour. You should stay out of this, Faye, or you may get hurt.'

His voice was quiet but there was an underlying thread of warning.

'Don't threaten me, Adam. I just want to know why you are doing this. And what does Natalie get out of it?'

'That girl is out for her own gain. She wants Luke and you're standing in her way.' He gave a low, cynical laugh. 'I don't care what the silly girl wants, she's welcome to him. As long as she does as I tell her, I don't care what it takes. Luke is not going to be top dog here when Monkshill is mine. He even took the woman I loved and married her. She got bored with him eventually and came to me, until the old man cut me off without a penny. Then she decided she wanted wealth more than me and wanted to go back to Luke. I couldn't let that happen!'

Faye's gaze widened in horror.

'You murdered her?' The words came out in a strangled croak.

'No, I didn't do it, although I felt like it, after she left me to go back to Luke!' he muttered with vehemence.

'But she was murdered, wasn't she?'

Adams gaze narrowed and he moved towards Faye.

'You want to know too much!'

She stepped back and was halted by a column. Fear was churning her stomach into knots.

She didn't really know Adam and what he was capable of. His next words answered her chaotic thoughts.

'I wouldn't like you to think I would stoop to murder. It was Natalie, driven by extreme jealousy who did it. She lured Helen to the ice-house on the pretext one of her cats was injured there. Natalie pushed her down the steps. Helen cracked her skull and died of a blood clot on her brain.'

Faye shivered with revulsion. She was aware of Natalie's dubious character, but to hear of what she had done was frightening.

'I've had my suspicions of her for several weeks, but I couldn't prove anything against her. I even told Luke, but he doesn't believe she is involved.'

'He's too trusting, always was,' he sneered. 'I'd be careful if I were you. Natalie has it in for you and you may end up like Helen!' He chuckled.

'You and Natalie are almost as bad as each other. What do you gain by disrupting Luke's plans for the house? Your father wrote you out of his will. There is nothing you can do to alter that!'

His hand reached out and softly stroked Faye's cheek.

'You are rather beautiful when you're mad.'

'Don't touch me!' She brushed his hand away, a look of distaste shooting arrows at him.

'My dear brother is not going to reap all the rewards while I have nothing! If I can't have Monkshill, then neither can he!'

Faye shrank back at the shocking threat in his tone. 'You're mad! I can't believe when we first met that I thought you were charming!'

'Just shows how wrong you can be!'

He laughed unpleasantly.

'Adam!' a voice called from nearby.

Natalie appeared from behind a cloister column. She scowled when she saw Faye, her eyes darting from one to the other suspiciously.

'I've been looking for you. What is she doing here? We can't risk letting her know anything.' There was panic in her voice.

'She knows nothing of our plans. What to do with her until we put them into action . . . now that is a problem. She must be kept out of the way.'

He rubbed a finger against his chin in thought.

'I know exactly what to do with her.'

Natalie caught Faye's arm in a vice-like grip, her eyes full of malice.

Faye struggled to loosen the girl's hold.

'You're mad, Natalie and you need help.'

'You'll be so sorry when I've finished with you!' she hissed. 'I know just the place where she can't spoil our plans, Adam. She can cool off in the ice-house.'

9

Did you put my cat in the ice-house?'
Faye asked Natalie, trying to stall for
time as she worked out in her mind
how to get away.

'You and that cat!' Natalie sneered.
'Of course I did. Anything to drive you
away from Monkshill!'

'Well, it didn't work, did it? And
whatever you are both planning will not
succeed. The destruction of the concert
stage was a pointless exercise. Luke can
take anything you throw at him.'

'Oh, my dear Faye, what we have in
mind next will be much worse than
that!' A fanatical glint lit Adam's eyes,
making her realise he had become
unhinged with mad hatred.

'Luke has done nothing to you, apart
from marrying the woman you wanted,
but it wasn't he who disowned you!'

'He could have reinstated me after

the old man died, but you know what he's done? Made out another will to leave Monkshill to charity!' Adam sneered.

'We're wasting time talking, Adam. Let's deal with her now! For a start she won't be needing this.'

Natalie ripped the mobile phone from Faye's waistband.

'Yes, we'd better get on with it. I don't care what happens afterwards. I will have had my revenge and there'll be nothing left for anyone.'

Faye felt a shaft of terror run through her. Was he intending to destroy Monkshill? She had to get away and warn Luke. Desperation threw her into action. She suddenly drew back her free arm and hit Natalie so hard across her face, the girl fell backwards. Faye took her chance and fled.

Adam cursed as he tried to catch up with her, but hampered by the monk's habit he wore, Faye was able to outrun him and put some distance between them. She glanced round to see him pulling the habit over his head and flinging it to the ground.

She was still some way from the house, but there was a small, wooded area next to the ruins and she ran into the shelter of the trees to hide. In the dark and in her haste, the branches and overhanging foliage, thick with centuries of growth, tore at her clothing and scratched her face. Her sweater became caught, losing her precious seconds while she struggled to free herself.

At last she was free and began to run as fast as she could. Then her way was barred by high, iron railings, stretching for as far as she could see in the pale moonlight. She suddenly realised where she was.

This was the Montfort family burial ground. For centuries they had been buried here and she recalled meeting Luke one day and he mentioned going to visit his parents' grave. Could she hide from Adam among the large monuments and somehow give him the slip?

She hurried on until she came to the gates. Would they be locked? No, she pushed hard and opened one side just far enough to slip through, carefully closing it to.

She hesitated for a moment. Had she the courage to go farther? Walking through a cemetery in the daylight was one thing, but in the dark and alone, Faye's natural fears began to surface as she moved farther among the gravestones, some of them Victorian monstrosities of gigantic proportions.

'Don't be silly,' she quietly chided herself. 'It's Adam who is the one meaning to harm you, not these long-dead people.'

Reassuring herself with those thoughts, she kneeled down behind a large monument, where she could have a clear view of the gates. The wait was long and Faye felt her bones begin to stiffen up. She was sure Adam hadn't come into the cemetery.

He hadn't been that far behind her and must have thought she had gone another way. She couldn't stay here all night. Luke must be warned as soon as possible. He would have to believe her this time!

A rustle in the grass nearby put her nerves on a razor's edge. She had a fear of rodents and had visions of mice running around her or worse!

She felt a shiver run along her spine at Adam's statement that Natalie had murdered Luke's wife, or as good as, if it was her hand which had pushed Helen. Did Natalie now see her as a threat to a possible relationship with Luke? If so she could be the girl's next victim?

She moved stealthily towards the gate and was pulling it open to slip through when an arm snaked out around her waist. Her scream was stifled by the hand clamped over her mouth.

'You shouldn't have come out of hiding so soon, Faye.' Adam's hot breath fanned her face. 'I knew you had come in here and I waited. You didn't know there was a gap in the railings farther down, did you?'

'Please let me go, Adam,' she pleaded, as he released his hand from her mouth.

'Let you go? So you can go running to baby brother, Luke? I don't think so. Don't be afraid, I've no intention of hurting you. Just a few hours in the cooler until I do what I have to and have time to get away.'

'You may not intend to hurt me, but Natalie has no such qualms.'

Adam twisted her around to face him, still maintaining his grip on her arms. 'Are you in love with Luke? If you are, God help you because Natalie won't let you live!'

'Yes, I am, but it's not reciprocated. Luke sees me only as a good employee.'

Adam's gaze roamed over her fair hair, made silver in the moonlight.

'He's a lucky man. I envy him. You've given your love to the wrong man, now you and I . . . ' He drew her close against him and bent his head until his lips touched her own.

She panicked and lashed out at his face.

'Why you little . . . ' Adam swore and lost his hold on her.

Faye took to her heels and ran, but she hadn't gone far before Adam's powerful legs caught up with her again. He knocked her to the ground and held her firm.

'This time you won't have the chance to run again.'

'How long do you think you can keep me a prisoner before someone misses me?' She tried to keep the rising note of panic from her voice.

'As long as it takes,' he muttered in a determined tone, dragging her to her feet. 'So help me, Faye, if you do anything foolish again I will hurt you.'

She was helpless against his brute strength. He dragged her along, skirting the wood. 'Please don't shut me in the ice-house,' she pleaded, genuinely afraid. 'I can't bear to be in closed places in the dark.'

'I'm sorry, Faye. It won't be for long.

Just a few hours until I've accomplished what I set out to do.'

'I feel sorry for you, Adam,' she said quietly.

'I've wasted enough time listening to you.' He dragged her even more forcibly forward.

As they neared the ice-house, Natalie appeared and ran to them.

'Thank goodness, I thought she must have escaped.'

'She did, into the cemetery,' Adam replied with a grim expression lining his features.

'I've got a score to settle with her for this.' She gingerly touched her face.

'Forget that now. We've more important things to think about.'

Faye almost slipped as the pair pushed her down the ice-house steps. The dank blackness closed around her when they opened the door and pushed her into the cavern.

'Have you brought a torch?' Adam asked and Natalie produced one from her jacket pocket.

'Give it to Faye!' he ordered.

'No, she won't need it.'

He stepped towards Natalie in a threatening manner. 'Give her the torch! It's bad enough being left here, but to have no light . . . ' He shivered visibly.

Natalie reluctantly handed it over. 'You're going soft, Adam.'

Her gaze returned to Faye. 'I vowed when Helen died no other woman would ever come between me and Luke. You will never have him.'

'Do you really think Luke will want you, Natalie, when he finds out what you've done over the years?' Faye cried. 'He'll turn from you in revulsion!'

'He won't find out because you will be dead before anyone finds you here. You'll freeze in a few hours. That's why they call it the ice-house.'

Natalie's laughter rose shrilly as she moved to the door.

'Promise you will come and let me out, Adam?' she begged before he began to close the door.

'I promise, before I leave this place for good.' He gave her a smile of regret.

The door closed with a hollow thud and the grating sound of the key turning filled Faye with a terror she had never known before. She flashed the light around the damp walls, feeling the coldness already begin to seep through her clothes. She wrapped her arms across her body, wondering how long this nightmare would last?

* * *

Luke was awoken by the shrill, piercing screech of the fire alarm. Darwin was pacing restlessly up and down the bedroom floor, going to the door and pawing to be let out.

Luke cursed and glanced at the clock as he sprang out of bed. Two o'clock. He'd only been asleep an hour. Quickly donning his clothes, he hurried on to the landing. There was no smoke there. He looked out of a window and saw with shock, flames billowing from the west wing.

'Oh my God, Faye!'

His heart thumped erratically with fear when he thought of the danger she was in. He went to the telephone in his bedroom and rang the fire brigade, then he rang Faye's flat number. No answer. He tried her mobile number, but it was turned off. Had the fire already reached her flat?

He ran out of the main entrance with Darwin at his heels and sped towards the west wing. The fire had caught in the middle section and he noted with profound relief it hadn't reached Faye's flat. Her windows were all in darkness. Hadn't she heard the alarm?

Thankful he had her flat keys attached to his own key ring, he ordered Darwin to stay on the path. He unlocked the outer door and raced up the stairs. Thumping on Faye's door brought no response.

'Faye!' he called after unlocking her door.

Lucy flashed by him and disappeared down the stairs. Smoke was now like a fine mist filling the air. Luke felt the acrid air affecting his throat.

The flat was empty. Her bed hadn't even been slept in. He knew she had gone to Scarborough for the evening with Josie. Had she decided to stay the night at her house? He hurried back down the stairs. Lucy mewed to be let out. He opened the door and she was gone, racing along the garden path.

If Faye's car was missing then he would ring Josie just to make sure she was with her. He raced to the garage and seeing her car was there sent even more dread through him. If her car was here where was she?

He was certain he'd heard her mention the fact she was picking Josie up and not the other way round. Was she wandering in the grounds, having heard the fire alarm? No, she wouldn't leave Lucy in the flat! He felt sick. Not just with worry for Faye. If the fire was the work of an arsonist, then he was sure this time it was Adam! He had sworn to get his revenge, but he had not realised how his brother's bitterness had turned to deep hatred until now.

He suddenly thought of Natalie. He hadn't seen her since dinner. She lived near to his own rooms and she surely would have heard the alarm. He went back into the house and climbed the main staircase, two at a time. Natalie didn't answer to his insistent thumping on her door. Using the master key he discovered she hadn't slept in her bed either.

Had Faye been right about Natalie all along? Was she involved with Adam? He hurried back to the ground floor and went outside. Darwin was lying on the lawn, waiting for him.

In the distance he could hear the fire engine sirens. At that moment there was a cracking, splintering sound as a window blew out and shattered with the heat, sending shards of glass everywhere.

He moved farther away from the

house and waited for the fire brigade to arrive. With a heavy heart he saw the fire had quickly taken hold. Faye's flat was now ablaze. If this was Adam's work he would never forgive him!

★ ★ ★

More than two hours passed before the chief officer pronounced the fire was safely out. Luke stared at the smouldering ruin which had been the west wing. It was entirely gutted.

Tears filled his eyes. Thank God his parents hadn't lived to see the desolation he was now facing, a large part of their beloved home destroyed. He turned away to try and block out the terrible sight. From the corner of his eye a dash of white ran across his vision.

'Lucy!' he called. The little cat ran towards him, then flew off again. He would have to try and catch her and take her to the kitchen. She could stay there for the remainder of the night.

When Faye turned up, she would be distraught if her cat was lost.

He began to call her, making soft, coaxing noises and feeling silly. Lucy came into view and padded towards him, warily. Luke bent to pick her up, but she was too quick and darted away again. This happened two or three times and Luke was about to give up, when he realised here was a pattern in her behaviour, as though she wanted him to follow her.

He could see her white form just ahead of him, but not near enough to catch. The abbey ruins were just ahead, but Lucy turned away in another direction, towards the wooded area where the deer roamed. Just like a feline she would stop and sniff at various spots along the way, but when Luke approached she would run farther on. Then she disappeared altogether.

'Where the heck is she?' He stood, mystified.

Lucy seemed to suddenly rise from the ground. In an instant, he knew where he was. She had come up the flight of steps from the ice-house! He cursed himself for not bringing his torch. Carefully negotiating the steps, he almost fell over Lucy at the bottom. She gave a loud meow.

'What is it, Lucy? What are you trying to tell me?'

'Adam! Is that you?' The voice came from the other side of the door and Luke thought he was imagining it above the cat's wailing noise.

'Faye! It's Luke!' He tried to push the door open.

'I've been locked in, Luke.'

The door was made of solid iron and her voice came faintly.

The ice-house had not been locked for years, so Faye must have been forcibly taken there to keep her out of the way, he thought, thumping his fist in frustration on the door.

'Are you all right?' he called.

'Yes, but I'm very cold. I've been here since about half-past twelve.'

'Don't worry, Faye. There is another

way out. I'll be about ten minutes, OK?'

Luke raced back to the house and found his torch. He hurried to the garage and saw the secret passageway door in the storeroom was open. He moved swiftly and surely along the tunnel, having knowledge of it all his life. He took the left-hand passage and before long he came to the door into the ice-house. The rusty key grated as he unlocked the door and pushed it open.

Faye was standing, focusing her torch on him, a look of fear widening her eyes.

'I've been going out of my mind wondering where you were, Faye!' He moved towards her.

'I was never so glad to see you, Luke!' Profound relief took the place of fear in her eyes, then she was in his arms, safe at last.

10

'I heard you call Adam's name. I didn't want to believe he could be capable of such despicable acts, but now I have to accept he is eaten up with hatred and jealousy.' Luke's breath stirred against her hair.

'Yes, he and Natalie forced me down here to keep me out of the way. He promised to return and let me out. They're both mad. I followed Natalie from the garage through the tunnel to the abbey ruins. I have so much to tell you, Luke, but we must hurry now. Adam is planning to do something terrible!'

Luke drew away and stared at her stricken features in the dim light from her torch. 'He's already done it, Faye. He's burned the whole of the west wing. It's completely gutted.' His voice was devoid of emotion and she sensed he was in deep shock.

'Oh, Luke, how dreadful! The whole of the west wing? My flat? Oh, my God, Lucy?'

'No need to fret. She's fine. I let her out when I was looking for you. If it wasn't for her you would have been in here a lot longer. She led me here.'

'She must have caught my scent in the grounds,' Faye whispered.

Luke put his arm around her. 'You're shivering. Let's get out of here.'

Together they walked back through the tunnel to the garage.

They went into the library and Luke poured brandy into two glasses, handing one to Faye. 'I don't think I know my own brother anymore,' he remarked as they sat in the comfy armchairs sipping their drinks. 'I was well aware he was angry at our father for disowning him, but to go to such lengths to gain revenge . . . ' Luke stopped speaking, feeling overwhelmed by the thought Adam hated him, when as children they had been so close.

'He believed you should have written him back into the will when your father died. He's furious you're going to leave Monkshill to charity.'

A disbelieving expression crossed Luke's face.

'I've no intention of leaving this house and estate to charity! Everything will be handed down to my children, if I have any.' He downed his brandy in one go, anger emphasising the gaunt angles of his features. 'What has Natalie got out of this? I treat that girl like a sister.'

'That's the problem, Luke, she doesn't want you to look on her as a sister. She wanted you as her lover.'

Luke gave a sigh of exasperation. 'I've never given her any encouragement in that respect. I've known her since she was a baby. Why would she want to destroy Monkshill?'

'Perhaps because she realised you would never love her in that way. She saw me as a threat and decided to help Adam as a way of getting back at us both.'

'Forgive me for not believing you about Natalie. I didn't think she was capable of such acts against me. I know this will devastate her parents.'

'It's hard to think someone close can betray you,' Faye murmured.

'The way I feel at the moment, I don't think I can forgive either of them, especially Adam, not just for destroying half our home, but for what he did to you.'

His gaze on her was intense and he was about to say further then appeared to change his mind.

'I have to go and look for Lucy.' She stood up and swayed slightly with tiredness. Luke immediately rose to his feet.

'Are you all right? You look exhausted. You stay here, I'll look for Lucy.'

'No, I'm just a bit tired. I must make sure she is all right.'

She moved to the door.

'We'll both look for her.'

Luke accompanied her out of the main entrance and on to the lawn. The blackened shell of the west wing stood out eerily in the moonlight, the air heavy with the acrid smell of burning.

'It's going to take me a long time to recover from this, Faye, if I ever do,' Luke said in a bitter tone. 'Adam knew by doing this it would destroy me, emotionally as well as financially. That wing of the house was our mother's favourite part.' The sharp planes of his features appeared carved from stone in the silver moonlight.

'He won't get away with it. The police will catch him and he'll be punished,' she replied in a quiet voice.

'You call a few years in prison punishment?' he scoffed. 'He won't have the lifetime of torment I will. I don't believe he ever really loved this place as I do. Years ago, before even my parents died he was talking of selling it to the National Trust, saying it was a millstone. Of course my father wouldn't hear of it and for his sake I knew when I took control of Monkshill, it would stay within the family.'

Something soft twined round Faye's legs.

'Oh, thank goodness!' she exclaimed in relief, bending down to pick Lucy up. She was rewarded with a loud purr, which reverberated in the still night. Luke reached out and stroked the silky head.

'I'm beginning to change my mind about the feline species,' he remarked. 'Lucy is the heroine of the night.'

'I'm glad. I think you've made a friend.'

She smiled as Lucy rubbed her head against Luke's hand.

'Shall we go in? It's been a long night for us all,' Luke said. 'I'll make the bed up for you in the room next to Natalie's. Perhaps there is some night-wear of hers you can use?'

Luke brought clean sheets and made Faye's bed while she looked through Natalie's things. She soon realised there were very few items left in the drawers and wardrobe. The girl had taken most of her clothes with her. There was a nightshirt and a couple of jumpers and slacks she thought might fit her.

She went back into the next bedroom where Luke had just finished making the bed. It was a large, pleasant room, but she was so tired she could have slept on a clothes line.

'Natalie's taken most of her things. Has she left in her own car?'

'No, I checked the garage after the fire engines had gone. Her car is still there. I expect she was too afraid to return to the house in case the police were here,' Luke said, deep in thought.

'She should have thought of the consequences before becoming involved in Adam's insane plans,' she replied without an ounce of sympathy for the girl.

It was past five o'clock when Faye said good-night to Luke and crawled into bed. Despite her chaotic thoughts she slept heavily until eight-thirty. Even Lucy did not prowl over the bed as she normally did. When Faye awoke and moved, Lucy padded up the bed and rubbed against Faye's face with her head.

'Is it time to get up, Lucy?' Faye groaned when she saw the time. She hadn't asked Luke whether he expected her to open the tea-room. She sprang up and hurriedly washed and dressed. She pulled one of Natalie's jumpers over her head and being a loose style it fitted her adequately.

Doris was entering the hallway as Faye came down the stairs. The housekeeper's face was pale with shock.

'I heard the news about the fire on the local radio and if Mr Luke hadn't rang me this morning I wouldn't have believed it! How did it happen?'

'We're quite certain it was started deliberately, Doris, but the fire brigade has a lot of sifting to do among the ruins yet.'

'Your lovely flat gone up in ashes like that!' Doris's expression was one of horror. 'Were you in bed when it started, love?'

'No, luckily I wasn't. I'll tell you

more later. Would you mind if I have my breakfast in the dining-room today?'

'No, love, you poor thing, losing everything. I'll bring a nice hot pot of tea and cook you up some bacon.'

She went away, muttering to herself about the ills of the world.

Faye went into the dining-room. She was surprised to see Luke there, thinking he hadn't yet got up. He was standing with his back to the room, staring out.

He turned and she was shocked by the haggard-look lining his features.

'Didn't you sleep well?' she asked, moving to him.

'About as well as you would expect. I had a couple of hours before the police called me at seven. Bad news, I'm afraid. There was a fatal accident the other side of Fossbeck. A car hit a tree head-on in the early hours. It took the fire brigade two hours to cut the two bodies out of the wreckage.'

'It's Adam and Natalie, isn't it?' She met his troubled gaze. He nodded. 'I'm so sorry, Luke. Whatever he did, he was still your brother.'

'Apparently the car had been speeding and must have skidded off the road. There were no other vehicles involved. Later this morning I have to go and identify the bodies.'

'I'll come with you,' she offered.

'Thank you, but this is something I must do alone. I'll put a notice on the gates to say we'll be closed for the foreseeable future. The Press have phoned already.'

'It doesn't take them long to start sniffing round,' she remarked cynically.

Doris entered, carrying the tray with the tea things. Faye went to take it from her.

'Would you join us in a cup of tea, Doris? I think you may need it. I've some bad news, I'm afraid,' Luke pulled out a chair for her.

Faye poured them all a cup of tea before Luke gave Doris the news about Adam and Natalie.

The housekeeper's rotund face fell.

'Adam, dead! I can't believe it!' Her features crumpled. 'It doesn't seem long since he were a little 'un, pinching my newly-baked cakes. He always had a bit of devilment in him, not like you, Mr Luke.'

'He had a lot of bitter resentment festering inside him, Doris. We think he started the fire because I wouldn't reinstate his position here after our father died.'

'He must have truly hated you, Mr Luke, to do that!'

She looked shocked.

'Yes, well it's all over now. I must ring Natalie's parents and offer them my sympathy.'

Doris sniffed. 'Well, I don't like to speak ill of the dead, but I can't grieve for that girl. She could be downright nasty when she had a mind to.'

Faye remained silent, listening, but she couldn't help agreeing. There had been nothing endearing about Natalie's nature.

Luke returned from viewing the

bodies later that morning. His bleak expression was enough to tell Faye it was indeed Adam and Natalie who had died in the crash.

For the next few days she hardly saw him while he was busy arranging Adam's funeral. At mealtimes he was quiet and withdrawn into dark thoughts of his own and Faye wished he would open his heart to her and allow her to share his grief.

After they attended Adam's funeral and the relatives and friends had left for their respective homes, Luke asked Faye into the library. He poured her a drink and seated himself in the armchair opposite to her. Darwin was lying on the hearthrug as usual, never far from his master. The rules on Lucy were now totally relaxed and the little cat had the virtual run of the house.

Luke gazed down at his whisky glass, wondering if he should get to the point immediately or lead up to it slowly and gently. Either way he knew it was going to be hurtful news for Faye and he hated himself for having to do it.

'Faye, there is no easy way of saying this, but I'm afraid I will have to terminate your employment. As you are aware, while the house and grounds are closed to the public the tea-shop will have to remain closed, for the foreseeable future at any rate. Without visitors the whole of my livelihood is in question. In short, I can't afford to pay your salary.'

'Couldn't you admit the visitors into the grounds only to see the abbey ruins and keep the tea-shop open? That would bring some money in. To help you, I would be willing to go unpaid until things are sorted out.'

'That's very good of you, but the police and fire brigade have told me I must remain closed until I receive the insurance money and the debris can be cleared. If anyone strayed too near the house it could put them in danger from falling debris. Insurers are not always quick to pay out. It could be months away. I have a manuscript at the publishers at the present time. I'm hoping they accept it as I have very little capital to live on. If not, I will have to end Doris's employment, too.' His sombre grey eyes swept over her.

She stared at him, inwardly pleading him not to send her away. If he didn't love her in return then it was better if she did leave, but it was breaking her heart to contemplate the thought.

'I don't know what to say,' she murmured. 'I love working at the Old Friary, but I understand perfectly why I can't stay.'

'Promise me you will come back once I get the tea-shop up and running again?' he asked.

'I can't promise, Luke. I have to look for another job and I may not be in a position to return here. When do you wish me to leave?'

Her voice broke with her unhappiness.

'I'll pay you two months' wages and it's up to you when you go. I'm not pushing you out, Faye. God knows, I don't want this. I've been more than happy with your management of the Old Friary and I thank you for that.'

Faye finished her drink and then made her excuses to go to her room. Once there she broke down in a flood of tears. To leave Monkshill and Luke was unbearable, but more unbearable was the thought he didn't love her.

11

Faye left Monkshill within the week. She knew delaying her leaving would only make it all the harder. As she said goodbye to Luke he had seemed cold and distant, and it wasn't until she was in her aunt's house in Hull in the privacy of her bedroom that she let the futile tears flow.

As the days passed Faye decided she wouldn't stay in Hull. The memories of the traumatic time caring for her mother were too upsetting. She decided to try and find work in Scarborough.

The fisherman's cottage she found to rent was up a steep hill overlooking the harbour. It had two bedrooms, kitchen, bathroom and cosy living-room, with a small garden for Lucy to prowl in. The view, especially at night, was superb when the whole of the bay was lined with glittering, coloured lights.

In no time, because of her catering experience, Faye found a job as a waitress in a fish and chip restaurant. It was only while the season lasted, but it would give her time to look for something more permanent.

The staff were friendly to work with and the owner, Jim Harrington, became in the habit of dropping Faye off at the cottage after work. Jim was in the throes of a divorce from his wife and Faye realised he was looking for another one, but she was trying not to encourage him. One evening he asked her if she would go out with him. Faye said yes. After all that had happened at Monkshill, she needed time to relax and revaluate her life.

They had a delicious meal in a hotel restaurant and spent the evening dancing. It was a long time since Faye had laughed so much and she began to wonder if going out with Jim would be such a bad thing after all. They had a lot in common and he didn't expect too much of her.

It was after midnight when Jim dropped her at the cottage. He drove off and Faye was unlocking her door when she heard footsteps come up behind her. She whirled, feeling alarmed, but the tall figure she knew so well was the last one she expected.

'Luke! What are you doing here?' She stared up into his taut features.

'Waiting for you. I'm surprised you didn't invite him in for coffee!'

His tone was sarcastic.

'It's the first time I've been out with Jim!' she replied sharply. 'How long have you been here?'

'I haven't been on your doorstep all evening, if that's what you mean. I happen to be in Scarborough for a one-day writers' workshop. I did come earlier and thought it better to return later, but I didn't envisage you would be out this late.'

She stared up into the shadowy chiselled features. 'Why shouldn't I be? I've had a very pleasant evening dancing.'

'You were the one who didn't yearn for the bright lights, remember?'

Faye was beginning to be annoyed by his caustic comments.

'It's very late, Luke, and I have to be up early for work. Can you please tell me why you are here?'

'I have some mail here for you. I thought, as I was in the town, it would be quicker and safer to give them to you. There is a letter from your solicitors. May I come in? I won't keep you long.'

'Of course you can, Luke.' She unlocked the door and led the way into the sitting-room. Luke glanced around the room appreciatively and moved to the wide window, staring out at the expanse of the bay.

'This is nice,' he murmured. 'We used to come to Scarborough for our family holidays when we were children and we stayed in places like this. Adam and I would . . . ' He suddenly stopped speaking.

Faye felt the sadness oozing from him

even though he hadn't turned round. Lucy padded across to him and rubbed against his legs. He bent down to stroke her, a smile dispelling his dark thoughts briefly. Then he straightened and his smile faded.

'Why didn't you let me know you'd moved here? I rang your aunt in Hull. She was surprised you hadn't informed me.' There was cold accusation in his tone and in the eyes which bore into her own.

'I am sorry, Luke. I intended to write to you. I've only been here two weeks and I'm just beginning to settle in my job.'

'What is your work?' he asked.

'I'm a waitress in a fish and chip restaurant. Jim, whom I went out with this evening, is the owner.'

'Bit of a come-down isn't it, after owning your own place and being used to the managerial side?' His tone was sneering.

'You sound just like Natalie!' she retaliated.

There was several seconds of icy silence.

'I'm sorry, I shouldn't have said that. What you do with your life is your own business.'

To break the awkwardness between them, Faye offered him a drink.

'I have no whisky, I'm afraid.'

'Tea will do, thank you.'

She moved into the kitchen. Luke followed and watched while she prepared the tea things. 'Did you enjoy the workshop?' she asked.

'Yes, but I don't wish to talk about that now,' he said rather abruptly.

Faye glanced at him, wondering why he seemed so ill at ease. She placed the teapot, milk jug and cups on a tray.

'Please excuse me for not helping you. I've had rather a lot of pain in my hands lately. I'm afraid I may drop the tray.' His tone was rueful.

'I understand, Luke,' she said sympathetically.

When they were seated, drinking their tea, Luke handed her the mail.

She glanced at the one from her solicitors.

'Do you mind if I open this one now?' she asked.

'I was rather hoping you would,' he remarked with a half smile.

A cheque was attached to the letter. She gasped when she saw the amount. Sixty thousand pounds! 'It's half of the money Tony owes me. The other half will arrive in three months time.' She handed Luke the letter.

'I'm glad for you, Faye. You've waited long enough for it. I knew if anyone could get things moving for you that firm would. What are you going to do with the money?'

Faye raised her head and stared at him thoughtfully. He had lost weight and there were dark shadows under his eyes. She suddenly knew what she was going to do with the money.

'I don't need it at this particular time, but you do, Luke.'

She rose to her feet and walked over to a small bureau.

'I'll give you a blank cheque and you write on what you need, all of it if you want. It'll take four days to clear.'

Luke got to his feet and catching her arm, turned her round to face him.

'No! I haven't come here for your money!'

'Why not? Call it a loan. You can pay me back when you receive your insurance money. Monkshill needs that money.'

He had tightened his grip and her body was touching his. The old desire for him was overwhelming her again.

'Forget about Monkshill!' he ground out angrily. 'I need you! Do you hear me?' He grasped her. 'I've been in torment since you went! I don't suppose you've even missed me!'

'Missed you?' She started at him open-mouthed.

It was too much temptation for Luke. His head bent and his lips met her own in a desperate kiss. She was so startled by his revelation she didn't respond at first. He drew away and held her at arms' length.

'Go on, sneer at me for the fool I am!'

His expression was dark with suppressed passion.

'You are a fool because you haven't guessed I've missed you more than anything, Luke Montfort. I love you, but you have never shown any sign my love was returned.'

'Of course I love you, Faye.' He swept her into his arms again. 'I was going to tell you when I kissed you in the library and Natalie interrupted us. I was so angry with her because the chance was lost. Come back to Monkshill with me,' he urged. 'I'm the most miserable man alive without you.'

She wound her arms around his waist and held him close. 'I can't put that burden on you, Luke. Not if you won't take the offer of a loan.'

Luke's breath stirred against her hair. 'I'm not asking you to return as my employee, my darling, but as my future wife!'

'Is that a proposal?' she asked, her

heart soaring with happiness.

'Yes, I'm asking you to marry me as soon as possible,' he asked, his mouth tight with tension.

'I will marry you, Luke, if you will agree to use some of the money to make Monkshill beautiful again and restore its dignity. There is nothing to stop us succeeding now in reversing its fortunes.'

The strain dropped from his features to be replaced with profound relief.

'You are right. Very well, I'll accept your offer and borrow some of your money, until the insurance pay up. The old house needs some happiness within its walls. When we are able to reopen the house and grounds, I'll leave it up to you whether you appoint another manager for the tea-room.'

She appeared alarmed.

'Oh, no, I love my work at the Old Friary. I couldn't bear anyone else to take over!'

Luke's expression was tender. He drew her closer and for a long time there was silence as they made up for lost time.

'Do you remember when I told you about Dominic?' His breath stirred against her neck. 'That those who see him never leave Monkshill and find their true love there?'

'Then I have a lot to thank Dominic for,' she breathed huskily, knowing she had found where her true happiness lay.

THE END